The Fantasy Horse

Jenny Hughes

The Fantasy Horse

Published by Pony, Stabenfeldt A/S
Cover and inside illustrations: © 2004 M. Stokes
Cover layout: Stabenfeldt A/S
Edited by Kathryn Cole
Printed in Germany 2005

ISBN 82-591-1175-6

Chapter One

I was running so fast I could feel the blood pounding through my veins and hear each breath my lungs expelled. I was nearly there, but I didn't dare look to my right. I just kept sprinting like a rabbit to the crumpled pile of clothes on the ground. I grabbed them with one hand, stepping rapidly into the skirt, pulling a lacy top over my head and finally forcing a gauzy white veil over the top of my hard hat. I flung my hand skywards to show I was ready and risked a quick glance at my rival. She'd been quicker, she was the best runner in the school after all, and she was already jumping up and down screaming encouragement to her approaching teammate.

But Robert was coming for me too. I could see his pony, Juniper, galloping flat out, neck outstretched. Robert, his long legs crouching in the stirrups, urged Juniper forward, as horse and rider drew closer. From the corner of my eye I saw a flash of bright chestnut, as the other horse reached my opponent. Then Robert and Juniper were at my side, wheeling in a brilliant turn as Rob spun his gray pony into perfect position.

"Emma, NOW!" he yelled.

I took a deep breath and vaulted, pushing both feet off the ground and springing upwards, swinging my right leg so I'd drop neatly behind Robert onto Juniper's strong back.

"Go, go, GO!" I needn't have shouted, Robert with the black coattails of his costume streaming in the wind, was already galloping in a straight line to the finish and we were catching up with the chestnut pony, then drawing level. For a moment the horses' heads were in nostril-flaring symmetry.

Juniper's speed began to tell and we were inching ahead, the roars of the crowd and our fellow teammates ringing in my ears as we pounded toward that finish line. And then we were over, a surge of sound met us and at last Juniper could slither to a halt and stand calmly, sides heaving. Robert and I jumped off immediately, hugged each other, hugged the gray pony, then hugged all three of us together.

"Photo! Photo!" Our team instructor rushed up, beaming and brandishing a camera. "Well *done!* We've won the cup for the third year in a row!"

"And we get to have a picture on record of Emma and Rob dressed as bride and groom." My friend Alice gave us a wicked grin as we smiled self-consciously for the camera. "Too sweet for words!"

"Unlike you," Robert retorted, tearing his costume off with what I thought was unnecessary haste. "Don't get any ideas of putting that photograph on the bulletin board will you, Alice?"

"It didn't enter my mind." Alice helped me remove my veil and "bride's dress." "Though everyone says you made a lovely couple."

"Stop teasing them, you minx." Alan Mathews, Robert's dad, was in the surrounding crowd. "Ignore her, you two. That was a great piece of riding. I don't quite understand the significance of the wedding theme …"

"It doesn't mean anything," I said quickly before anyone started any more jokes about Rob and me. "It's just a Pony Club thing, you know, a dress-up game when one team member rides to the rescue of another. Sometimes they get you to do it as dragons and maidens in distress."

"Well, it's my first experience of the Pony Club Games Championship and I'm very impressed." Alan patted his son's back proudly. "I'll leave you to collect your cup and celebrate, then I'd like a word with you both, if that's okay."

"Sounds serious." Robert loosened Juniper's girth and raised his eyebrows at me. "I wonder what he wants."

I was too busy getting Rocco ready for the presentation to wonder. My beautiful black pony had performed brilliantly throughout the contest, galloping and turning, bending and spinning, and if all the other ponies in our club team had been as good, we'd have won the cup by a mile instead of just those last precious points. I gave his gleaming ebony shoulder a final brush and hopped into the saddle, ready to ride into the ring. Robert and I led the team. At nearly fifteen we were among the oldest and longest serving, having ridden with the club for over six years. He and I had liked each other immediately; we were both highly competitive but enjoyed a good laugh as well, and even at age eight we'd kind of gelled right off the bat. I suppose that's why we were being teased so much about the bride and groom game, and although I denied the whole idea as quickly as Robert did, a part of me quite liked the notion of our friendship developing into something deeper.

Still, this was no time to get soppy as Juniper and Rocco, their necks curved in perfect, proud arcs, walked together to halt before the Pony Club dignitaries. A big, cheerful man made a very nice speech, congratulating the whole team on our performance, and only spoiled it a bit as he handed over the hefty silver cup by saying, "To the most talented and attractive bride and groom we've ever seen." I blushed, and when I looked at Robert he was grinning affectionately at me so I blushed even harder. The team did the traditional lap of honor with Rob and I holding the cup with one hand each between our two horses. Rocco, being so clever of course, knew we'd won and really played to the crowd, swishing his tail and prancing showily.

"Go on, Emma." Robert smiled at me as we neared the exit. "Take him into the center and let him do his stuff."

This next part makes me sound like a real show-off, but I knew everyone loved to see my pony do his act, so as Robert and the team left the ring I curved Rocco away and cantered in a diagonal line across the grass. Rocco, his ears pricked, kept a smooth pace as I double vaulted from side to side, then he spun in a perfect turn on the forehand as I asked him to rear, lifting his forelegs and pawing the air like a wild stallion. I know it's not part of Pony Club training, but I discovered Rocco loves to learn all sorts of tricks since he came to me as a green young horse four years before. Now the crowd cheered and cheered as he stood on his hind legs in a perfect classic pesade, dropping down to extend his off fore and bow deeply, touching his nose to his knee in a beautiful,

8

graceful thank-you. I bowed too, and then we cantered away, with my pony giving one saucy high buck as we finally left the ring, which made everyone roar with laughter.

"You're a couple of real stars, you two." Robert was watching, still with that look of fond pride and Alice pointed at him, making mock swooning motions and kissing sounds.

"Shut up you." I slid off Rocco's back and handed her his reins. "If you've got so much spare energy you can make yourself useful and start getting him ready for the trip home."

"Yes your majesty, your very royal highness." She mucked about, bowing and groveling till Robert pretended to boot her out of the way.

"She's a complete nut, your friend," he told me. "But if she really is going to untack Rocco for you, we could go over and see what my dad wants."

"Okay." I'd rather have stayed and cuddled my pony but I could see Rob was eager to find out what was going on.

Alan was sitting on the grass, talking animatedly into his cell phone, but he switched it off when we arrived.

"I got you some drinks." He opened a couple of cans. "I still can't get over how terrific you two were."

"It's a good team." Robert took a swig.

"Oh sure, but you and Emma in particular – just fantastic!"

"Thanks, Dad. Maybe you wouldn't sound so surprised if you came along to the competitions a bit more often."

10

"Yeah I know Rob, but it's difficult. What with the divorce and my job taking me so far away – " Alan looked harassed and I felt sorry for him. "Your mother tells me about your riding and, well, that's part of the reason I'm here. You know the park we've been working on?"

Robert had told me the company his dad worked for had designed and built a fantastic new theme park somewhere up north.

"It's nearing completion and the publicity people are putting on a huge spectacular for the opening. It's an adventure-based park as you know, and the finale of the show's going to be a battle built around the Fantasy section, rival tribes on horseback, that kind of thing."

"Sounds good." Robert coolly took another swig. "What's it got to do with us?"

"The promotion company has employed a director, actors, and professional stunt riders, but they want talented kids to take part too. I heard them say they were recruiting from Pony Club teams so I thought of you immediately – and Emma, of course."

"And our horses?" I was really, *really* excited at the thought, but wouldn't even consider it without Rocco.

"Definitely. Talented, well-trained ponies and riders, that's what the director's looking for. So you'd be interested, would you?"

"You bet – " I began but Robert broke in swiftly.

"Maybe. What exactly would we have to do? And when? We've got school, remember."

"Of course you have." Poor Alan seemed disappointed his son wasn't more enthusiastic. "The opening's mid-August, the show runs for seven nights and they want ten days rehearsal, so it's all happening in the holidays.

Your mom says it's okay with her if you want to do it. Look, I've got all the details." He produced a folder. "Have a read through with Emma and let me know to-morrow."

"In a hurry, Dad?" Rob took the folder but didn't open it and his father sighed.

"I only heard about the recruitment for young riders yesterday, and I thought it would mean I could see a lot more of you for a few weeks. If you don't like the idea, don't worry." He got up and walked away, hands pushed deep in his pockets.

"You were pretty rough on him, Rob." I leaned over and grabbed the papers. "It sounds fabulous. Hey! Listen to this!"

Robert sat moodily while I read out a description of the place we'd be staying – a brand-new Gothic-style ho-tel in the park, while our horses enjoyed acres of fine grazing. It seemed we were to spend most of the day thundering around doing amazing riding, making new friends, and meeting celebrities. I stopped for breath and looked at him.

"It *sounds* all right," he said reluctantly and I hit him with the folder.

"All right? All right? It's fantastic that's what it is. Oh, come on Rob, lighten up! I thought you liked your dad. Why are you giving him such a hard time?"

"I haven't seen much of him since he started this job, and I thought – I thought maybe he couldn't be bothered with me."

"Duh! The park's hours away and it's been an inten-sive project for him – look at the size of it! As soon as he heard something that meant you could be there too, he rushed down to tell you." I could see Robert needed it spelled out for him. "It was lucky we were taking part in the Pony Club Games. He could see right away what a great rider you are."

"And you." He gave a fainter than usual version of his cheeky grin. "So you think you might enjoy spending a couple of weeks in a fabulous hotel in an new theme park do you, Emma?"

"Um, let me think." I pretended to hesitate for two seconds. "D'you know, I think I could live with that! As long as you and Juniper and Rocco are there too."

"Same goes for me." He fell back on the grass and suddenly yelled, "Whoo-hoo!"

I did the same and we rolled around laughing, so that by the time we got back to our horsebox we were covered in grass, and of course, everyone started joking about that too! I was pleased that Robert seemed pretty unconcerned at the ribbing and just kept all fingers and toes crossed that he wouldn't change his mind about taking up his dad's fabulous offer. I told my own parents about it as soon as I got home; it had practically eclipsed the excitement of winning the Pony Club Games Cup, although I was still pretty thrilled about that. Once my mom and dad had phoned Rob's mother to find out all the details, they were totally cool about letting me go, especially when they were offered tickets to the opening night show. I couldn't wait to tell Robert.

"Yeah, my mom thinks it sounds okay too," he said.

"Okay? Okay? It's – it's – " Words failed me and that doesn't happen often. "Phone your dad up *now* and tell him we want to go."

"Nah, I'll wait till tomorrow." He seemed determined

not to show his father any enthusiasm and I couldn't understand it.

I didn't push it though. Robert and his dad were obviously struggling a bit with their relationship, and it wasn't up to me to tell Rob how to act. I was nearly climbing the wall with frustration the next day though, waiting to get the definite go-ahead. At last Rob turned up, very monosyllabic about the conversation he'd had with his father, but at least I heard the word I'd been dying for.

"Yes? We're going to be stunt riders? Oh, WOW Rob!"

"I don't think stunt riding is exactly what we'll be doing. They've got professionals for that and proper actors for the main roles. The Pony Club kids take the part of two warring tribes, we all ride on dressed in costumes, and there are chases and battles and stuff. But guess what? Dad videoed us yesterday and showed the director. He immediately said you and I were good enough even though he didn't get to see the show you and Rocco put on at the end."

I was glad he'd only seen the "bride and groom" race and said so. "He'd have thought I was a little show-off if he'd watched us collect the cup, but it's great he realized how good Rocco and Juniper are. Did he say anything else?"

"Yeah, and I think you're going to like this too. He says he can take one more pony and rider – all our team looked good, but he wanted a colored horse, piebald or skewbald, doesn't matter which."

"Paint!" I shrieked. "That means Alice gets to come along!"

Paint is Alice's terrific black and white pony, and the

thought of having my best friend join in the forthcoming fun put the icing on the cake for me. Now all I had to do was get through the last few weeks of school and the three of us and our beloved horses would be off for the adventure of a lifetime!

Chapter Two

To say the time dragged slowly is like saying double geography is not the favorite period of my timetable. Stating the obvious or what! I drove everyone around me nuts and they were all highly relieved that at last the day came when the horsebox arrived to collect Rocco, Juniper, and Paint. It was followed in short order by a coach for Robert, Alice and me. We were the first three passengers, but as we drove north, the large bus soon began to fill up with chattering, laughing kids from different Pony Clubs in the region.

"They're all pretty hyper." Robert looked around us. "Though no one quite as much as Emma."

I elbowed him but I didn't mind really. I didn't think I could *get* any more excited, but when the coach finally drove through huge gates with "ADVENTURE WORLD INC." carved in big curly letters above them, I was very nearly sick. We entered via a wide, sweeping driveway, curving uphill as far as the eye could see.

"Look, Em," Alice pointed to our left where the gigantic towering figures of a man in a space suit and an incredible green alien faced each other menacingly across an entrance.

"Space World," Robert said casually. "My dad designed a lot of the stuff in there."

"Cool!" Alice and I were terribly impressed and gazed with added interest at the amazing planet towers, spaceship tracks, and monster aliens we could see from the window.

Space World covered acres of ground, as did the Computer Heroes section and the very, very spooky-looking Horror World.

"That's where our hotel is," Rob told us. "But Dad says we're getting a quick tour around Fantasy Land first, to see what it's all about."

What can I say? It was truly, truly – *fantastic!* I suppose the rides were similar to ones you've probably been on elsewhere, a log flume plunging into a deep pool of water, things that whizzed you around, turned you upside down and spun you sideways, terrifying great poles with circular cages that dropped like mighty stones into caverns below ground, but everything *looked* so stupendously different from anything we'd ever seen. It's hard to describe – the mystic landscape dotted with iridescent waterfalls and glittering rocky outcrops looked as if it had come straight from the pages of a compelling fantasy storybook. Weird, misshapen trees with gargoyle faces rattled their branches beneath the skeletal arms of metal stanchions that formed the framework of the rides. Dominating the area was the colossal track of the biggest roller coaster you've ever seen. There were no passengers yet, of course, but the carriages were hurtling above, below, and around us, like bullets of gold, silver, and bronze.

Robert cleared his throat and tried to speak in a normal voice. "Everything's going to be switched on to show us what it'll be like when the park's opened. It's – it's pretty impressive, don't you think?"

Alice and I just nodded dumbly, trying to take it all in. A loudspeaker crackled suddenly and a booming voice told us Fantasy Land was based around the mythical tale of two warring tribes, the invading Zardonnes and the heroic Sushawny. Each ride represented the struggle between the two clans and the huge roller coaster illustrated the final battle for power. There was an audible intake of breath; the whole coachload gasped in unison as the background behind the giant ride came to life with hordes of galloping computer-generated horses plunging and rearing around it. The effect was breathtaking. Even from down on the ground in the confines of the coach, it seemed as though we were being swept along with the warriors and their fantastic horses, whose long, wild manes and tails were shot through with strands of scarlet, emerald, and sapphire. Above the apex of the ride a black and silver horse reared, his diamond-bright hooves flashing as he appeared to strike out at the bullet-shaped cars that would soon be carrying park visitors. Seen from the dizzying heights of the roller coaster itself, the effect would be completely mind blowing.

"Okay, everyone." The loudspeaker voice became suddenly normal. "We hope you enjoyed your brief look at Fantasy Land. We're now going to show you the arena where you'll be doing your riding action, which will be a real-life enactment of the story you've just seen. Afterwards, you can relax in your quarters or go and greet your horses. Welcome to you all."

"And to you, buddy," Alice said agreeably and every-

one laughed, glad to have the electrifying atmosphere created by Fantasy Land lightened by a nice mundane remark.

The grassy area designated for the show was enormous, a great circle of turf where carpenters were busily erecting a complex stage while others worked on tiers of covered seating. Perched at the top of Adventure Land's hill, the surrounding view was amazing, as trees and grass fell away, displaying a panoramic view of the whole park with Space World, Computer Heroes, Wild West, Fantasy Land, and others spread in dazzling array below.

"Awesome," Robert muttered and I squeezed his hand to let him know I was proud and grateful his dad had made us a part of this experience. After our tour, the hotel we were ferried to came as less of a surprise than you'd think.

Normally, if you found yourself lugging your suitcase up the black marble steps of a four-star version of Count Dracula's Gothic castle, you'd pinch yourself to see if you were dreaming. Now we took it completely in our stride. Alice and I were sharing a room, I was glad to discover. Despite it being hung with black drapes and gossamer fake cobwebs, it was extremely comfortable. Rob went off to find his room, arranging to meet me in ten minutes so we could go and find Rocco and Juniper. In fact, I just threw my bag on one of the beds, and feeling I just couldn't wait any longer to see my beautiful pony, I was banging on Rob's door about a minute after he'd walked inside.

"You and that horse of yours." He pretended to groan but he followed me back downstairs right away.

Because our coach had taken a while to pick everyone up, the horsebox had arrived well before us, and we rushed through the spooky woods in the direction we'd been told. I was really glad to see that once we'd left Horror Forest, as it was called, the landscape became much more normal. Rob said this was because several acres of grass had been left for future expansion, which, now that they'd been safely fenced, were perfect for housing the fifty or so horses and ponies being used in the show. The organizers had sensibly divided the fields into paddocks, and when I saw the gleaming ebony lines of Rocco, head down as he contentedly grazed with his pals Juniper and Paint plus a little group of showy ponies, my heart lifted.

"He looks fine!" I said with relief, and Robert threw back his head and laughed.

"Of course he does. What did you expect – that he'd be lying down in a sad little heap? Rocco can actually survive a few hours without you, you know, Em!"

"Bet he missed me though." I climbed over the fence and gave a low whistle.

Rocco's head came up immediately and he whinnied, calling my name, I liked to think. Soon we were enjoying a cuddle and a sharing a few tidbits while I checked him over carefully.

"You've got to be fit for your first day's work tomorrow," I told him, rubbing his velvety ears. "You just won't believe what we're going to be doing, Rocco!"

Robert had let Juniper go back to his grazing and was giving Paint a going over. "Alice will be too busy making new friends to come out here for a while," he told the piebald. "So I'll make sure you're okay."

21

"Hey, you two!" My friend's voice carried clearly across the field. "I wish you'd waited for me," she was grumbling as she came over to join us. "Coming through that creepy forest by myself is just not my idea of fun."

"Wait till they switch the special effects on." Robert laughed at her cross face. "Dad says they've got bats that flit around outside the hotel windows and some of the trees come to life and stomp around. It's just for visual effect from inside – after we've gone the guests won't walk through the woods, of course."

"Just as well." Alice draped herself over Paint's back. "I'd have died if one of those grim-looking trees had moved."

"Or a bat landed in your hair." I pretended to swoop at her head. "What a fantastic place though, Ali – just awesome!"

"Amazing," Rob agreed, sounding quite proud, I thought. "I suppose we'd better get back and see what's happening."

"We all have to meet in the dining room," Alice said, unwinding herself from her pony. "We get fed, obviously, and also get to know the rest of the guys. The ones we met on the bus seemed nice. I hope the others are too."

We went back inside to find out. There were forty or so, mostly around our age or a bit younger, and like us, most of them couldn't wait to get started on the rehearsal.

"If the battle scenes projected around the roller coaster are anything to go by, it's going to be sheer mayhem." Trudy, a very pretty girl with waist-length blonde hair had joined us right after we finished eating and was making quite a play for Robert's attention. "When do we find out if we're goodies or baddies, Rob, do you know?"

"Tomorrow, I guess." He didn't seem particularly impressed by all the hair tossing and eye contact. "Baz, he's the director, will have it all worked out, I imagine."

"So is Baz one of your daddy's friends?" Stuart, tall, dark, and scowling seemed to follow Trudy wherever she went.

"No, my dad's only met him once or twice I think," Rob said mildly.

"Oh, what a shame. Does that mean you won't get a starring role?" Stuart was obviously jealous of Trudy's flirting and was getting plenty of digs in.

"Doubt it." Robert looked a bit puzzled, not having worked out why he was being given a hard time. "They're using real stars, didn't you know?"

"Yeah we heard that," a tall, skinny boy called Darren said. "Who are they?"

"Well, there's Troy Mitchell for one – " Robert began but was drowned out in a barrage of girlish shrieks and screams.

"Troy Mitchell!" Alice rolled her eyes theatrically. "You didn't tell us that, Robert! He's the most gorgeous thing on TV. I've had his poster on my wall for months – I can't believe I'm going to get to meet him!"

"You'll see him, but I don't know about anything else." Robert was bored with all the squealing. "I think he plays the son of the Sushawny king – that's the good tribe – so maybe if you're on their side, Troy will get to boss you around."

"Anytime he likes!" Alice said fervently and all the girls agreed with her.

I wasn't too bothered. I don't watch much TV and haven't even seen the teen series that Troy Mitchell stars in, so I didn't care if I was in the same tribe or not. Being a goodie means you get to win, I figured, but it might be more fun to be a member of the war-like Zardonnes. Robert's dad had given him a lot more detail than the rest of the kids had, and he spent most of the evening answering a million questions. Alice and I had tried one of the Play Stations, taking on Darren and a cheerful guy called Fox. Every time I looked around I noticed Trudy hadn't moved from Robert's side and that Stuart was looking even more morose. It was really noisy. Forty kids playing music and games or just talking made for decibel-busting volume, and I was quite glad when a staff member came in and clapped her hands for silence.

"Early night for you all, if you don't mind." She smiled in a steely kind of way that didn't invite discussion. "We aim to start as soon as it's light, and you and your ponies have to be ready. Apart from your usual riding gear leave everything else here and make sure you remember your room number. It's too complicated to issue you all with keys, and it shouldn't be necessary – security on the site is very strict, so no outsiders can get into the hotel. Any questions?"

A great barrage of hand waving and yelling erupted but she staved everyone off by saying, "No, not about the rehearsal – Baz will explain all that in the morning. Just practical stuff – no? That's good. See you all at breakfast, which is at 5:30."

"I didn't know there *was* a 5:30 in the morning," Alice moaned and I laughed at her.

"It's the best part of the day; you'll love it, Ali."

I thought that with all the excitement none of us would ever get any sleep, but very soon the lofty "castle" was still and quiet. The only sound I heard as I drifted into sleep was the distant hooting of an owl. I wondered dreamily if it was a real one or, like so much in this strange new world I'd entered, a complete and utter fantasy.

Chapter Three

There was no doubt about it being real first thing in the morning. I started off gently shaking Alice, saying softly, "It's nearly 5:15. Time to get up."

Her only response was to burrow deeper under the blanket so I shook a bit harder and spoke louder. This time she grunted but stayed hidden, curled up like an oversized hamster in its nest.

"Come on, Alice." I took a firm grip and tugged at the bedding, making her squeal and burrow even further. "Alice, get *up*!" I was practically yelling, but it still took another five minutes to dig her out of that bed.

We eventually arrived in the dining room about 5:40 with Alice stumbling blearily, but at least dressed and conscious. The first thing we saw was Trudy, immaculate in show riding gear, her long hair in a shining braid, talking animatedly to Robert.

"What's *she* doing at our table?" Alice muttered and I shrugged resentfully.

"Hi. Morning." Trying to be mature about it I sat down opposite the two of them and poured out some orange juice. "Here you are, Ali, it'll help wake you up."

She planted herself down and took a slurp.

"Oh dear, not morning people, I see." Trudy smiled at us sweetly, no doubt taking in our slightly scruffy appearance, dressed, like everybody else, in our everyday riding clothes.

"You could say that about Alice." Robert smiled straight into my eyes. "I bet it was hard work getting her here, wasn't it Emma?"

"Pretty tough." I grinned back, glad our close, easy relationship seemed exactly as usual. "I've been awake for hours already. I'm so excited about riding today."

"You're gonna love it. Emma's a fantastic rider, and her horse, Rocco, is a complete star too," Robert told Trudy, and I thought her smile became a little thinner.

"Nice," she said distantly. "Wait till you see Giselle. She's a gem."

Giselle, her own pony, was a palomino, and once everyone was mounted and ready, the two of them were easily the most glamorous. A very attractive red-haired girl named Ginny owned the showy chestnut that was sharing our paddock, but even they couldn't match Trudy and Giselle for sheer good looks. Trudy's appearance didn't worry me; I'm not usually the jealous type, but I felt if she kept chasing Robert so blatantly, I could make an exception in her case! The atmosphere was fantastic; we were all raring to start rehearsal, so when a stocky, leathery-looking guy rode over and announced there'd been a hitch, we all gave an enormous groan of disappointment.

"Sorry, kids." He was looking pretty tense. "The plan was to take you straight to the arena, but overnight some of the staging collapsed so there's a lot of repair work going on. Baz asked me, I'm Jim by the way, to start things off in one of the fields, so if you'll all follow me."

"At least we're going to do something." Alice was still in early-morning grump mode. "There's no way all the grooming and stuff I did should be wasted."

Jim opened the gate into another of the paddocks, where staff was rushing around putting out marker cones and erecting a couple of small hurdle fences. Despite the last minute change of venue it was all very well organized. We were issued with colored and numbered bibs, half red and half blue.

"There's no significance with the grouping at this stage," Jim told us. "It's just so we can differentiate between you all when the action starts."

He swung down from the big bay he was riding and sent us across to the marked-out ring to do some warming up exercises. Rocco, like me, was very excited at being part of such a big group of ponies and had been prancing and pulling like a train, but now that he saw he was expected to do some work, he calmed down and started concentrating. We started with simple flat work in walk, then at working trot, changing reins and diagonals across the ring. Jim stood in the center calling out commands while some of the other stunt riders and staff watched with hawk-like intensity. Once the horses were warmed up, Jim had us cantering circles and serpentines and jumping the hurdles. It was all pretty basic stuff and by the time he called for a break, I couldn't help feeling a little disappointed.

"Look at Emma's face!" Robert teased gently. "Bit of an anti-climax is it, Em?"

"Well, yeah," I admitted. "I thought it was going to be a lot more exciting."

"Just you wait." Fox rode over on his skewbald mare,

28

Gabby. "I've been talking to the professional stunt riders and think Baz has got some brilliant plans for us."

"Really? Did they say what kind of thing?" I asked eagerly.

"Lots of charging around, swooping down to pick up spears at a gallop, jumping weird obstacles, weaving in and out of trees …"

"That sounds more like it." I was all fired up again.

"Baz will be along in a minute. He'll assess our riding and sort us into tribes, but you can bet whatever happens, all the tall guys will be in the Zardonnes."

That meant Robert would definitely be amongst them, and he looked at Fox in surprise.

"How come? I didn't see anything about height in the Fantasy."

"It's nothing to do with the story – it's just that Troy Mitchell isn't very tall himself, so Baz doesn't want the Sushawny prince being dwarfed by his followers. He's going to pick a really pretty girl to be the prince's companion as well, and the guys have taken bets that'll be Trudy."

"She's nowhere near as pretty as Emma," Robert said immediately and I felt myself go gooey inside, but was too embarrassed to show it.

"Don't be nuts," I said. "Trudy and Giselle look perfect for the part. I'd rather be a Zardonne with you anyway; it sounds like more fun to be a marauding bad guy."

An excited murmur swept through our crowd as a jeep could be seen heading in our direction, swerving as it approached fast over ruts in the field.

"Baz is coming!" everyone said as we all stood there, holding our ponies' reins and gaping at the oncoming jeep, eagerly waiting for our first glimpse of the all-powerful director. I nearly giggled when the jeep stopped and a short, round man bounced out looking more like a beach ball than the creative genius we'd been told to expect. Appearances, of course, can be deceptive and we quickly learned that the small Baz had a very, very big personality. Within minutes he had everyone organized, telling us he wanted to see us all within various small groups and then as an entire "tribe," defined for now by the color of our bibs. We were to canter, then gallop into the ring, listening for his instructions as we did so.

Our horses, nicely warmed up and responding to the buzz of excitement we were all feeling, entered into this with great enthusiasm. Our numbers and colors were called, seemingly in no particular order, as Baz, armed with a megaphone, told everyone what to do. I heard my call – red number seven – and moved Rocco forward, cantering easily to join five other riders as we entered the marked-out area. We had to canter in unison to the center X, and then divide into two groups, one peeling off to the left and one to the right.

"Meet at point A, ride to X as one group, separate again with each group jumping a hurdle simultaneously."

It was still pretty simple stuff but getting the instructions right, coping with very excited ponies, and keeping together as a reasonably united group, made it interesting to say the least. Rocco, of course, loved it, changing legs and adjusting his pace perfectly when I asked. Although I made a total mess of our approach at the first jump, we kept going and our group left the ring feeling quite relieved. Baz had high standards and obviously expected the forty horses and riders to perform their varying routines perfectly, but ponies and kids being what they are, there were the occasional blunders and near disasters.

I worried a bit about Alice; she's a terrific rider but prone to lose concentration. In fact she managed all of her sessions really well. To my surprise Trudy was one of the worst offenders, getting in such a muddle when she was supposed to gallop a diagonal from K to M, picking up a stick from a bucket en route, that she actually lost her way completely, forgot her stick, and ended up practically knocking Baz off his rostrum. Darren was another one, managing to crash his chestnut pony, Socks, *through* the small hurdle instead of over it, after which he promptly fell off and let Socks run amok till the other riders in his group managed to catch him. Despite these hiccups, Baz seemed to think it a reasonable demonstration and after a longish pause, he called us all back together.

"Jim will let you have more details later, but briefly, after conferring with my staff and stunt guys, this is how it's going to look for our first proper rehearsal. I'll read out the twenty names who'll be taking the part of Zardonnes and of course, the rest of you will be Sushawny."

He reeled off the names and what do you know – Fox had been right. Robert, Stuart, and all the other really tall boys were named in the first twenty. Trudy, the stunt riders' favorite to be a Sushawny princess, was also in the baddies group, but she made a point of smiling sweetly at Robert when her name was called, so I guessed it was okay with her and felt another stab of resentment. Ginny,

31

the tall, pretty redhead looked delighted when Baz announced she'd be "junior leader" of the Zardonnes and would be riding with their king and prince. Then – I clearly remember the amazement I felt – he said, "And Emma Jessop on her black pony Rocco, will be doing the same with the Sushawny Tribe. That's it, everyone, two hours lunch break rest for your horses and then we hope to take you across to the theater arena for our first run through."

He bounced back into his jeep and was driven off, again at great speed, leaving us all in a noisy group as we talked about the morning's happenings.

"I didn't think I'd get picked at all." Alice took off her hat and shook out her sweat-dampened hair. "Half the time I just galloped like a mad thing copying everyone else."

"It's lucky you didn't copy me, then," I laughed. "I thought I was terrible."

"You looked good though," the lanky Darren said gloomily. "I'm the only one who managed to fall off, and I did it right in front of Baz, too."

"Our horses crashed shoulders when we went over," Fox grinned. "So we were lucky our group of riders didn't all hit the ground at the same time."

"And I started bombing off completely the wrong way." Stuart was looking really hot and bothered. "But Ginny yelled just in time so I didn't make a total idiot of myself."

"I hope you're not saying *I* did!" Trudy gave him a furious look and he crumbled immediately.

"No, course not, Trudy. Giselle – um – bolted, didn't she? Not your fault at all."

"Huh!" She turned her back on him. "My pony will be

better once I'm riding with you, Robert. Juniper's so calm and you're so masterful."

Rob looked highly embarrassed and tried to ignore the black look he was now getting from Stuart.

"What about Emma?" he smiled at me. "I said it would be you they chose for the Sushawny princess, Em."

"It's not a princess – I'm not – " I muttered, feeling very self-conscious. "I just get to ride up front with the prince that's all."

"That's *all*, she says." Alice gave me a good-tempered shove. "You get to be up close and personal with Troy Mitchell, that's what it really means. Some girls have all the luck!"

I grinned and hugged Rocco, glad we'd done so well, but still feeling that I'd much, much rather be riding with Robert than with some hyped-up TV star who'd probably turn out to be a complete and utter pain!

Chapter Four

I realized I'd be an idiot to turn down a prime riding opportunity like this, so I put up with all the leg-pulling about "heartthrob" Troy and just looked forward to finding out what Baz had planned for Rocco and me. All the ponies were untacked and given a small feed and we were told while they rested that we could either go back to the hotel for lunch, or get something at the caterer's station near the theater arena. Our group, Robert, Alice, Fox, Ginny, Trudy, Stuart, and I opted for the theater choice, hoping for a good look around. There was a great spread of food set out in a marquee, but to our disappointment we weren't allowed into the arena because the construction crew was still having problems. Fox managed to get a chat with his stunt-rider friends and came back to us with the update.

"They've managed to fix the damaged stage, but we can't get into the arena because they've had to take all the seating apart and it's spread all over the place. Apparently the fixing bolts they used are the wrong size and the seats could be dangerous. Till the right ones arrive, they can't have fifty horses rampaging around the place."

"Oh no! Does that mean the afternoon's rehearsal is cancelled?" I asked.

Fox shook his head and grinned at me. "Keen to get going, aren't you, Emma? I think we're returning to the field we used this morning."

This was fine by me, but Trudy pulled a petulant face.

"I don't like it there, I think they should wait till we can use the proper arena."

"That's stupid," Robert said. "As long as we're learning what to do and practicing how to do it, I don't see a problem. It's not as if we will be using the actual stage; all our battles and stuff take place on the grass in front."

"No, I agree with Trudy," Stuart said immediately and wicked Alice muttered, "Well there's a surprise, everybody!"

Fox heard and laughed with her, but pointed out it didn't really matter what any of us thought because any decision would be made by Baz alone. He was right – as we were leaving the marquee a harassed-looking man rushed over and told me that Rocco and I were required on stage in an hour while the others were to be mounted and ready in the field.

"That means I don't get to see you anymore today, Emma." Robert looked annoyed.

"Sure you do. I'll probably only be a short time, but even if I'm here all afternoon, we'll meet up at the hotel."

"My dad's taking me out right after rehearsal," Rob said moodily. "He wants to spend some time with me, or so he says."

The others had walked on ahead and I stopped for a moment and stared at him, feeling puzzled.

"You still don't believe him? Why would he bother to get you here if he didn't want to see you?"

"I don't know." He looked suddenly vulnerable. "Since he and my mom broke up it all feels different."

"I know, and it's a shame, but stuff like that happens all the time. You just have to believe your dad still feels the same way about *you*."

"It's hard though, Emma."

"Oh come *on,* you two." Trudy had started walking back toward us, and I said a very rude word under my breath.

I could see Alice and Fox giggling as they watched Stuart trotting to catch up with Trudy. I sighed inwardly, wondering why life had to be so complicated!

"Thank goodness for you, Rocco," I told him as I got him tacked up again. "Sometimes people are just too confusing!"

Our riding instructions, when we got them, seemed comparatively simple.

"You're to enter from the left at canter, veering in a semi-circle to approach the stage," Baz told me. "The king will be seated on the second level and you'll ride alongside Rick on his black horse and slightly behind Troy, who's riding a white pony. You halt on the grass, then in turn get your horses to ascend two steps onto the first level of the stage. There will be some dialogue ending with Troy saying, "Sire!" and bowing. He then rides across the stage, descends the steps on the far side. Rick bows to the king and follows. Then you bow and follow, and all three ride off to the right. Got that?"

I nodded and he looked skeptical. "Let's see you do it then."

I moved Rocco away from him, riding behind the towering structure of the stage. The crew working on the seating was a safe distance away, so I turned Rocco smoothly and asked for canter. He flowed into the three-beat time and we rode in a perfect curve toward the steps where we halted, allowing time for the two other riders to move first. I then urged my clever black pony forward and he walked confidently up the two steps and stood on stage, both of us turning our heads to the throne where the king would sit. I didn't know how long the dialogue would take but after a while someone called, "Sire!" to give me the cue and again I gave enough time for Troy and Rick to do their exit routine. I could tell Rocco was enjoying himself. He loves anything new, so when I felt it was my turn, I made a sweeping bow and asked my pony to do his, feeling his muscles bunch as he extended his off-fore and touched the knee with his nose. I heard Baz chuckle, a rich, throaty sound of pleasure, as we trotted smartly across the stage, down the steps and cantered off to the right. Jim was there, and as I came toward him, he gave me a spontaneous round of applause.

"Perfect, Emma! Troy has been trying to get that right for ages and you've done it in one go! Well done, girl."

I smiled my thanks and took Rocco out to the front again. Baz was on his rostrum, bouncing up and down with enthusiasm.

"Excellent – um – Emma, excellent. Do it for me once again and I can bring Troy and Rick in and get this blasted scene out of the way."

"Was Rocco's bow okay?" I asked rather timidly knowing he hadn't actually asked for that.

"I loved it, and I think the crowd will too, but I'll double check to make sure it doesn't upstage Troy."

I wondered if the actor demanded a say in every aspect of this production, thinking if so, he was going to be even more of a pain than I'd anticipated. I did the routine again and Rocco performed perfectly, much to the delight of Baz.

"Back you go again, and we'll try it with all three of you."

This time when I rode Rocco backstage a short, dark-haired guy was there, sitting astride a stunning black thoroughbred.

"Good work, Emma." He raised his hat in a nice old-fashioned kind of gesture. "I'm Rick and this is Tsar. We're number one stunt riders here, but I can see we'll have to work hard to stay that way with you and your horse around. What's he called?"

"Rocco." I patted him proudly. "So, where's Troy Mitchell?"

"On his way." He pulled a face. "He's a nice enough kid and a good actor, but a rider he isn't."

I was starting to dread meeting this temperamental star and felt quite gloomy as the showy white lines of a gray pony rapidly approached. I knew what Troy looked like of course, having seen his face on a hundred magazine covers as well as Alice's bedroom wall, so the fact he was good looking didn't come as a shock. What I hadn't actually expected was that he'd be *that* great close up, and I'd seriously underestimated the charm in that well-known wicked smile of his.

"Whoa, Crystal." He brought the gray to an untidy halt and I got the full impact of blue eyes, blond hair, white teeth, and general drop-dead gorgeousness.

"Hi." He leaned over and kissed my cheek. "You've

39

got to be this incredible Emma everyone's talking about."

"Hello. I suppose I am." I said faintly.

"And you really did that whole entrance/exit thing for scene five right off the top?"

"Scene five?" I must have sounded a complete moron. "Oh, the steps and the bowing? It's Rocco – he's really clever."

"Well good for you Rocco, my friend." Troy talked clownishly into my pony's ears. "Just have a quiet word with Crystal, would you? She and I aren't exactly doing what we're here for, and we're driving Baz crazy."

"It's not just you." Rick did a few warm-up dressage steps with Tsar. "There are lots of things going wrong that are interrupting rehearsals; that's what's really driving him nuts. Ah, here we go. They're calling you, Troy. We're right behind you."

Troy nodded and quickly put Crystal into canter with Rick and I on our two black horses moving smoothly behind him. The entrance we made was okay, though Troy rode a rather uneven and jagged semi-circle and when he came to a halt he'd put Crystal at an odd angle, making it hard for her to walk neatly up the steps. She made a reasonable attempt and stood quietly until Tsar and Rocco were on the stage behind her. Troy glanced quickly at Baz then, half turned toward where the audience would sit on opening night; he began his speech to the king. He had a beautiful voice that carried powerfully, and the stirring words sent quite a shiver down my spine.

"Sire!" he ended, bowing deeply, his hair gleaming like burnished gold.

It was impeccably done and a great shame that what

should have been a regal, imposing exit was distinctly marred when he put Crystal all wrong again at the far end of the stage and the poor mare slithered and scrambled down the steps onto the grass. Baz threw down his script and practically howled. "You make it look as if you're riding a disabled camel, Troy. Watch Emma and see how she does it."

Rick stood aside and Rocco and I made our bow, crossed the stage and stepped perfectly to the ground.

"There. How hard can that be? Just do it – oh, what *now*?"

One of the crew had run over to him and was talking urgently.

"Get Emma to give you some tips," Baz bawled as he jumped irritably off the rostrum. "I have to sort out another problem. I want this right when I come back. Rick, come and give me a hand."

So now I had to give the "star" riding lessons! Despite Troy's undoubted good looks I wished miserably I'd had the sense to turn this part down. He must have a monstrous ego to think himself capable of riding this role and I didn't particularly like him *or* the thought of teaching him.

"I might be able to help," I said diffidently. "I'm sure Crystal can manage it. The problem is …"

I was going to say, as tactfully as I could, that he needed to get the horse in the right position and on the correct leg, but to my great surprise Troy gave a big groan and said, "The problem is – the horse is great but I'm crap. *That's* the problem."

"I wasn't going to say that," I tried again but he gave me a pale imitation of his fabulous grin.

41

"Don't worry, Emma, you don't have to be kind. Believe me, no one else is – Rick's completely given up trying to put up with me. The only way I'm going to be any good in this part is not to ride at all. I should have told Baz I'm a complete novice instead of swearing I could do it."

"You can do it and you *have* to ride," I argued. "The whole fantasy is set around these warring tribes of brilliant horsemen. You can't be the Sushawny prince and not ride. It's like – it's like –"

"Doing a Grand Prix story and not driving, or an opera and not singing." He gave another rueful smile and I distinctly felt myself warming to him.

"You can ride okay," I said encouragingly. "Well, good enough for most of the stuff Baz wants. I don't know about the battle scene ..."

"Baz has already arranged it so my big fight part is done mostly on foot. It'll still look good – we go up and down all the different levels of the stage and I get to swing across on a rope and everything."

"So it's mostly entrances and exits?" I was sure we could work it out. "Let's start with this one, it's all a question of timing, I promise you."

He'd been sitting despondently on the grass but he climbed gamely aboard Crystal and followed me back to try again.

I found that by breaking the action down into small components, Troy gradually learned exactly when and how to position the gray horse correctly. She was a willing, well-schooled pony and by counting out the paces and getting Troy to strike off correctly, we eventually managed a complete and perfect run through. We were just in time. Baz came back looking like thunder, hopped straight back up on his rostrum, and demanded to see what progress we'd made. Rick and I got into place and followed Troy as he plunged in the curving semi-circle toward the stage. It wasn't quite as smooth, but it was pretty good and a smile at last lifted the down-turned corners of the director's mouth.

"Good. Much better Troy, thank you. And thank you, Emma."

Rocco and I made our bow in reply and Baz gave that lovely, rare chuckle. He still had a lot of problems to sort out he told us, but said if we could spend the rest of re-hearsal time perfecting Troy's entrances it would at least make something a success. I was quite happy with this. The more time I spent with Troy the more I liked him, though I still wasn't interested in him at all. But I thoroughly enjoyed my day and didn't really give much thought to all the things that were going wrong around us until I got back to the hotel. There it couldn't fail to hit me – all hell was breaking loose, kids shouting and crying and even, I was told, parents on the phone demanding their sons or daughters return home immediately!

Chapter Five

Being the last one to arrive back, I didn't have a clue what was going on.

"Alice?" I ran up the stairs and looked into our empty room.

"She's with Fox; his is one of the rooms that got robbed," Ginny called out, and I raced down the hall in the direction of her voice.

"Robbed?" I couldn't believe it.

"Yeah, six or seven rooms were trashed and money got stolen."

"No!" I stared at her. "Is everyone all right?"

"Just fuming mad mostly, though a couple of parents have reacted pretty strongly. They don't like the idea of their kids staying."

"It'll mess up rehearsals really badly if we start losing people," I said, wondering how Baz would react at yet another disaster.

"Oh, I think it's all under control now. We're to hand in any cash or valuables and they'll be put in a safe till we want them."

I thought that made more sense than issuing door keys that could easily get lost or stolen. Ginny and I made our way to Fox's room, which was on the next floor up. The Gothic flavor of the hotel was carried everywhere, I noticed, with spooky suits of armor, fake arches and beams, and beautiful, gloomy sculptures and carvings. There was a huge round window on one of the landings, made to look like the web of a giant spider, and I could imagine how amazing it would be to peer out and see the gruesome moving trees and fluttering bats in the surrounding Horror Wood. Not to everyone's taste I guess, but Rob had told me there was also a space-themed hotel plus a regular one. Adventure World was certainly trying to cater to everybody! Poor old Fox, when we reached him, wasn't in the mood for appreciating any of the décor. He and Alice were tidying his room, scooping armfuls of stuff off the floor and into closets. Darren was there too, grumpily hurling his own stuff into a suitcase.

"You okay?" I asked Fox sympathetically. "No one got hurt, I hope."

"Nah. They think it must have happened either at lunch time or just before the majority of us got back tonight," Fox said. "No one saw a thing, but someone must have sneaked past the security guys, otherwise it means one of us Pony Club kids is responsible."

"My parents say that's ridiculous." Darren moodily inspected his Walkman. "They say unless they get more assurance we're safe here, I'll have to go home, so I'm packing just in case."

Having seen his feeble attempt at hurdle jumping, I privately felt we could easily manage without him. If he took Trudy as well, it would be just perfect!

I said impatiently, "Of course it's safe! I'm sure Fox is right and it's just a one off – somebody managed to get

past the guards when they weren't looking. What do the police say?"

"They're not that interested, apparently." Alice shut a drawer with a loud snap. "It's Adventure World's problem, I guess."

"Along with everything else that's gone wrong." Ginny looked worried. "You don't suppose there's some sort of jinx, do you? The stage collapsing and the seats being wrong, and now this?"

"I don't know about the rest, but thieving can't be because of any jinx." Fox ran a hand through his sandy hair. "And if I find who stole my spending money, I'll gladly set him straight."

The talk during our meal and for ages after was all about the thefts, but gradually everyone simmered down and started discussing the day's rehearsal. It sounded as though they'd all enjoyed it, but of course all of them, well all the girls anyway, wanted to hear about Troy Mitchell.

"What's he like?" Alice pretended to swoon. "I mean, *really, really* like?"

"Nice," I said cautiously.

"Nice! Nice! A – a cheese sandwich is *nice* – we're talking gorgeous Troy here."

"Maybe he's not so great in real life." Trudy shook back her hair. "He's probably got pimples and bad breath."

"No he hasn't got either," I said quietly and Alice pounced instantly.

"Hah! You got real close, didn't you, Em? Don't tell me he kisses you! As the prince I mean."

"I shouldn't think so. I didn't get to see the whole

play. We only practiced entrances plus one scene where Troy spoke to the king and three of us rode on and off the stage."

"You did that all afternoon?" Ginny sounded surprised. "We didn't have the director of course, because he was with you, but the assistant went through a lot of stuff with us."

"Wait till you get Baz," I told her. "He wants everything exact, precise, and perfect. You'll go over the same thing a million times."

"That doesn't sound like much fun." Stuart was Trudy's shadow as usual. "He seems like an odd little guy too. I can't think why everyone seems to jump when he says jump."

"He has that strong kind of personality, and because he's a perfectionist and knows exactly what will look good, it makes you want to get it just right," I tried to explain. "He's taking the riding rehearsal tomorrow, so you'll see what I mean."

"Yeah, yeah." Alice, like a dog with a favorite bone, wouldn't leave the subject that interested her most. "Who cares about Baz? What I want to find out is how Emma knows Troy doesn't have smelly breath. You don't find that out just trotting and cantering around. You two got personal, didn't you?"

"No." I could feel my face getting hot. "It was just riding like I said. But – well he did kiss my cheek when we met. That's all."

"If that had been me I'd never wash my face again." Alice pretended to faint on Ginny's shoulder and they both fell on each other, giggling.

"If you ask me Troy Mitchell sounds a complete

creep!" Trudy, obviously resenting the attention I was getting, shook her hair around even more. "You should be careful, Emma. You don't want him making a complete fool of you."

That made Alice and Ginny roll around with laughter again, so Trudy flounced off angrily, followed as usual by Stuart. As soon as they'd disappeared some of the other girls started making meowing noises and saying what a jealous cat she was.

"Now ladies!" Fox came over and grinned mockingly at us. "Don't be nasty, we all have to stick together, you know. We don't want any fighting offstage – we've got enough of it when the Sushawny meet the Zardonnes."

"I hope you've noticed how the baddies have been saddled with the two worst riders," Ginny complained. "We've got Trudy *and* Darren, so that gives you Sushawny a head start in the battle."

"Yeah, those two will either fall off or get lost on the way." Alice was still chuckling, but she tried to stop when Darren came walking toward us.

"Hi," Fox greeted him. "Did you manage to calm your parents down?"

"Yeah, they've agreed to let me stay, so I've unpacked again." Darren didn't look particularly thrilled, I thought.

The rest of the evening was pretty uneventful, except that Trudy remained in her huff and wouldn't have anything to do with us. I was really glad to see Robert arrive and even more pleased to see him head straight in my direction. I thought he wouldn't have heard about the thefts, but he said he'd been told when he came back to the hotel after rehearsal.

"I only had a few minutes to get showered and changed," he said. "So I didn't hear any details. How much was stolen?"

"Quite a lot of cash; we all left our spending money here, so whoever it was got away with a fair haul. Security says that no one except authorized people, that's the staff and us basically, came into the hotel. It must have been an inside job."

"That's a nasty idea." Robert thought for a minute. "When we came back into the park, Dad showed me around Space World, which is fantastic, but he had to show his official pass about four times to have us admitted, so I guess it *would* be hard for an outsider to get in anywhere."

I was fed up with talking about it. "How did you get along with your dad?"

"Okay." He immediately looked guarded and I sighed. "You're not still giving him a hard time are you, Rob? He's doing his best after all."

"Yeah maybe." It was his turn to change the subject. "How did your rehearsal go? You didn't go all weak in the knees when you met Troy did you?"

"No!" I decided against telling him about the kiss. "He was all right, but he's a complete novice at riding."

"Really?" Robert was quite amused. "Strange casting then, wasn't it?"

"I don't think Baz realized how inexperienced he is, and anyway, they booked him for his big name I guess. Troy said he was really eager to play the Sushawny prince, so I think he might have exaggerated his riding prowess."

"Cheating little sneak! And *is* he little? Short I mean?"

"He's taller than I am," I said, "but not as big as you. He liked Rocco, though. He said so."

"Oh well, he must be all right then!" Robert was teasing me, having seemed to relax now he knew I hadn't been bowled over by the TV star.

I noticed Trudy hanging around a couple of times, but for once she didn't come over and try to monopolize Rob. I was really pleased she'd decided to remove herself from our little crowd. Once again we were asked to make an early start the next day, at the same time getting a speech about the thefts and the new security measures that would be in force. We were given big envelopes and told to put all our cash and valuables in them, labeled clearly, so they could be kept in the safe. I did mine before we went to bed, but Alice couldn't be bothered. After the usual battle to wake her up in the morning, more time was wasted while she blearily collected her money and wristwatch. It meant we were late for breakfast, and my heart sank when I saw that not only was Trudy sitting at our table again, but she was looking very smug and self satisfied. Robert, on the other hand, was obviously in the blackest of moods, scowling angrily as he chomped on his toast.

"Good morning, girls," Trudy said, but I ignored her and spoke straight to him.

"What's the matter, Rob?"

"I need to talk to you." He got up abruptly and stomped across the room. I followed till we were clear of the tables, then grabbed his arm and said "What *is* it, Robert?"

He spun around, his eyebrows drawn in a straight, angry line. "Why didn't you tell me Troy Mitchell kissed you?"

51

Inwardly I cursed myself for keeping quiet and not realizing that the blonde girl would be bound to make a big deal of it. "I didn't think anything of it. It didn't mean a thing."

"You said it was so good you'd never wash it off!"

"No I didn't. That was Alice being silly." I was starting to get annoyed.

"Yeah, right."

"Yeah," I repeated strongly. "Absolutely right! Don't believe Trudy over me, Rob. You know I'm not swooning over Troy."

"I don't *know* anything," he said moodily.

Although I felt sorry he was feeling so insecure, I wasn't going to put up with this kind of nonsense so I said, "Use your brain then, and work it out. I'm going to get some breakfast."

I walked quickly back to the table, aware that he wasn't following, and thought grimly that I'd enjoy telling Trudy just what I thought of her, but she, too, had gone. I managed to force down some food, then dragged the still half-asleep Alice out of the hotel to start getting the horses ready. I was to spend the morning rehearsing with the rest of the tribe and while I wanted everything between Robert and I to be okay again, I was still angry that he'd believed Trudy's lies and felt they'd both be in trouble if I got the chance to get my revenge on the battlefield. As it turned out, there wasn't much opportunity for any contact. Baz was in charge, and he went through our entrance in such minute detail that we didn't get to the battle proper, at least not officially. Baz started by telling us about the rehearsal procedure.

"Those of you who've never had any theater experience might find all this very confusing to begin with," he told us. "We don't start at the beginning of the story and work through to the end, at least not yet. What I intend to do is take a particular scene and work on your element within it. Yesterday, amongst other things, my assistant got you started on the final scene of the Fantasy and I want to tweak and hone that performance until it's perfect. Briefly, this scene leads to the climax, which will feature Rick and his horse, Tsar. Rick leads on the Sushawny, followed by Jim, then Emma riding Rocco. The Zardonnes enter with stunt riders Dave and Mike, followed by Ginny on Firefly. This is to be a dramatic entrance. Each tribe will ride up the hill on either side of the stage so that the audience will see a moving line of horses and warriors surrounding the arena on the brow of the hill. The riders I've named gallop forward, stunt riders performing Cossack-style vaults. Then they swoop down to pick up a sword each, followed by the entire tribe. There will be fantastic music and lighting effects, but I want the audience to gasp when they see *you*. Okay, we'll try that – get into your places and remember! You're not just riders, you're warriors and you're full of passion!"

Well, I thought, putting Rocco into canter as we moved back to prepare for the start. *With the mood I'm in that's one thing I'm definitely full of. You want passion, Baz, well here we come!*

Chapter Six

I thought we were brilliant. Rick and Jim checked that we were all ready then swung into action, the beautiful black Tsar and Jim's imposing bay horse galloping with long, smooth strides as their riders double vaulted across the grass. Our ponies, with their shorter legs, surged energetically after them. At the point where a cylindrical drum filled with sticks had been placed, Rick and Jim swung dramatically from their saddles as they swooped down with their free hands to pick up a sword from the grass. Leading the other riders as instructed, and maintaining the fast pace, I leaned forward, grabbed a stick from the drum and galloped on, hearing the pounding hooves as the rest of the Sushawny followed.

Rocco was having the time of his life and thundered onwards toward the "battlefield" where he mingled and cavorted with the leading horses of the Zardonnes who reached the spot slightly later. The sticks we'd grabbed represented the swords we'd be getting later, and some of us had an enthusiastic time bashing the opposing tribe with them. I was busy looking for Trudy to give her a whack when I became aware of the noise Baz was making through his megaphone. And not in a good way, I might add, as our director's view of our first attempt wasn't anything like mine. Far from finding us brilliant, he seemed to think it was the worst entrance ever made and we had to separate into our two tribes once more, go back down the hill and start all over.

The work on the stage seemed to be finished, but the crew was still laboring on the seating, having tidied everything into piles out of the arena itself to make it safe for us to rehearse. And rehearse we did. Baz said most of the individual riding performances were fine, but he wanted the overall picture to be of tightly consolidated units, horses and riders flowing in synchronized movement.

"Doesn't want much, does he?" Fox said wryly. "I'm sure that last time was practically perfect."

I'd thought so too, but Baz, frowning on his rostrum, didn't seem to agree.

"It doesn't have enough impact." He suddenly bounced away and picked up a marker cone, waving at some of the crew to help. "Take a break, everyone, while Rick and I try something out."

I slid off Rocco's back and gave him a huge cuddle. He was loving every minute and hadn't even started to sweat, because although the pace was fast, we were only doing short bursts of action. The other ponies were quite relaxed as they dropped their heads and nibbled the sweet, lush grass. Alice and Fox flopped down next to me.

"Are you enjoying it, Fox?" I was impressed with Baz's high standards, but realized not everyone was going to feel the same.

"Oh sure, it's good fun, but I don't see how we can improve the routine much more."

55

"Me neither," I agreed, but pretty soon we were called back and given new instructions.

"It looks great with the two lines of horses appearing over the hill," the director said. "But the gallop forward is too simple. I want the audience to see the skill and commitment of the tribespeople."

Fair enough, I thought, but blinked a bit when he told us what he wanted now. We were to enter in two lines as before, but instead of riding in single file to pick up our swords, one rider from each end of the line was to curve away, then race between twin sets of bending poles (they'd be disguised as exotic fantasy trees, Baz said) reaching the drum exactly together to each pluck a sword and gallop in pair formation to the battle site. Rocco and I love bending races, but the thought of keeping perfect time with another rider in a parallel line was challenging to say the least. We tried it several times, some more successfully than others. I was smugly delighted that our tribe, the Sushawny, were a lot better at it than the baddie Zardonnes. Trudy got herself into a terrible mess, twice galloping Giselle to the wrong set of poles and clashing horribly with Stuart who was trying to navigate them on Drummer. Busy as we were with our own practice, we could hear Trudy's voice raised in complaint, and since I hadn't forgiven her for stirring up trouble for me, I couldn't help laughing. Darren and Socks were creating problems too, and I felt sorry for Ginny who was trying to make some sense out of the havoc. Baz, would you believe, was happier.

"It's a total mess at the moment, but keep working on it and it'll look fantastic."

"I think he must be seeing it from an artistic point of

56

view," I said to Alice and she giggled and said we certainly wouldn't win any Pony Club prizes.

I'd finished my umpteenth attempt and was waiting on the battlefield for the rest to join me. We weren't allowed to do the "sword fighting" again (apparently we were to have separate lessons at that), I looked around at where the audience would sit. It certainly would be a breathtaking spectacle from their viewpoint, provided we ever got it right, and I was amused to see several of the crew stop their seat building to watch us. One tall, lanky guy was looking at Baz as if he couldn't believe his eyes, and I grinned to myself before I turned away to lead my tribe back to the start. This time the skewbald, Gabby, expertly ridden by Fox, stumbled slightly and knocked a pole. This meant Rocco and I got ahead and arrived at the drum way before them.

"No! *No!*" Baz yelled. "Emma, I expected better of you. Do it again!"

"Oh, do it yourself if you're so clever," I muttered, and turned my pony away, just as a tremendous crashing and clattering sound echoed around the arena. All the horses jumped, startled by the frightening sound. Giselle, who'd been nearest to the seating, panicked completely. Trudy, waiting in the center, had been watching the others and was caught off guard as her pony half reared, snatched at the bit, and bolted. To her credit Trudy managed to stay aboard, though thrown out of the saddle and without stirrups she did well to hang on, regain the reins, and bring the palomino to a safe halt.

"What the heck was that?" Baz ran toward the crew while Robert rode Juniper quietly over to join Trudy.

I knew he was being kind and practical, using his

horse's calm presence to help soothe the frightened Giselle, but I felt suddenly lonely, abandoned, and very, very jealous.

Baz, meantime was giving the crew absolute hell. A pile of seats and their metal fittings had been knocked over, sent flying from the top of the stands to the bottom. No one, it seemed, knew exactly how it had happened. After firing a million questions Baz picked up one of the fallen seats and waved it menacingly at the entire work force. We couldn't hear what was being said in reply, but the body language of the crew said it all. Hunched, irritable, puzzled, and frustrated – they all appeared deeply resentful and Alice, for one, could understand why.

"It was just an accident; no need for Baz to give them such a hard time over it."

"On its own it's a minor happening," Fox agreed. "But to Baz it's one more near-disaster in a whole line of disasters."

"If more of the horses had panicked it could have been really nasty," I said. "Still, I see that Trudy's making the most of being comforted by Robert, so she didn't do too badly."

The blonde girl was practically resting her head on Rob's broad shoulder, and I felt another crippling surge of jealousy. Baz came back toward us, obviously full of pent up fury and frustration. He made a visible effort to calm down before going over to Trudy to ask if she was all right. She immediately stopped doing the poor little girl act with Robert and put a brave smile on her face.

"I'm fine, thank you, Baz. It's just lucky I know how to handle a bolting horse, isn't it?"

I saw Robert shake his head at her blatant change of

attitude and was glad when he turned Juniper and left her happily describing the way she'd coped. I was even more pleased when he walked his horse to me, raised his eyebrows, and said, "More drama! D'you suppose Baz will give the lead role to Trudy now that she's told him how wonderful she is?"

"Maybe." I looked directly at him. "Unless he realizes she's not that concerned about telling the truth."

"Ouch!" He grinned at me and I felt the lost, lonely sensation slipping away. "Okay, I get the point. I'm sorry I believed her."

"So you should be." I slid down from Rocco's back to give him a rest and decided to be kind to Robert as well. "D'you want to get a soda while they decide what to do next?"

"Sure." He hopped off Juniper and we started leading the two horses to the refreshment stand.

As we walked I became aware that a great stir of excitement had begun amongst some girls who were ahead of us.

"Troy Mitchell!" one of them shrieked. "There he is – look!"

It was the first time they'd seen him in the flesh, of course, and their voices got higher and higher when they realized the TV celebrity was actually approaching them.

"Hi." He was hidden from my view behind the crowd of girls and their ponies, but I could hear his voice quite clearly. "One of the guys just told me there's been some sort of accident – seats collapsing and a horse bolting? Do you know who got hurt?"

They all answered at once, a babble of excited voices

each giving him different information, and as Rob and I got closer, I could now see Troy's bewildered face as he tried to take in what they were saying.

"So nobody got hurt? And – " He suddenly spotted me through the crowd and the glow in his blue eyes instantly deepened. "Emma! You're okay! I was so scared you and Rocco might have been hurt."

The look on the other girls' faces as he strode forward, put his arms around me, and hugged me to him was priceless, but I didn't want to think how Robert would react. I soon knew though. Before Troy had even released me, Rob had swung back aboard Juniper and was cantering away, coldly ignoring both of us. Troy didn't seem to notice, he was now patting Rocco with what seemed the same amount of relief and affection, and had no idea of the rift he'd just reopened between Robert and me. I ended up silently drinking my soda while Troy good-naturedly signed autographs and chatted to his adoring fans. One of Baz's assistants came over and gently reminded the girls they weren't supposed to bother Troy or the other actors, adding that they might as well take their horses back for their lunch break, meeting up again in the rehearsal field.

"Baz has decided not to use the arena till everything's finished," he told Troy. "He can't risk another accident and says you and Emma were going to work up here this afternoon, but you'd better find a quiet corner somewhere else instead."

"No problem." Troy never seemed to get difficult or temperamental as I'd imagined he might. "Is that all right with you, Emma? We could use that small field over there."

"I'll take Rocco back for his rest and meet you there at two o'clock," I agreed, getting back into my saddle.

Alice and Fox had already untacked Paint and Gabby when I reached them but there was no sign of Robert. We'd been planning to use the couple of hours off to explore some of Adventure World's delights, but I felt sick with frustration that Robert wasn't going to come with us. It was turning into a day of disappointments. As we left the paddock, a security guy told us we weren't allowed anywhere in the grounds.

"New instructions, I'm afraid," he said. "There are concerns over the source of these so-called accidents and management doesn't want you kids anywhere you can't be supervised."

"Supervised!" Fox said in disgust. "You'd think we were six years old!"

"What other accidents have there been, anyway?" Alice wanted to know. "There was the thing this morning, and the stage collapsing, but you can't call the thieving at the hotel an accident."

I wondered if there had been more problems than we'd heard about and made up my mind to ask Troy later. He'd been here rehearsing much longer than we had, and would likely know. We spent a fairly dull lunch at the hotel only lightened by the news that, because our movements within the park were so curtailed, the coach would be available every evening to take anyone who wanted to go into the nearest town. I told Troy when I saw him, but he shook his head.

"It's better than nothing, I guess, but you'll be limited in what you can do because you'll have to be back here early."

"I think I'll go anyway," I said. "I'm beginning to get a bit stir-crazy stuck in here."

He laughed in the nice, friendly way he had, and I thought it was a good time to try finding out how much he knew about what had been going on. It turned out he knew a great deal, and he was completely open about it.

"The problems just keep on building up. Right from the start things went wrong, incorrect equipment, like those seating bolts arriving, or stuff going astray. Baz says everyone kept blaming the production company, but all the records show things are being done properly at that end. It seems to be Adventure World that's at fault."

"Is the rest of the park having trouble too?"

"I don't think so. Most of it's nearly complete and running pretty smoothly from what I've heard. It's everything to do with the Fantasy play that's going wrong – the big spectacular opening that Adventure World wants so badly."

"Maybe someone doesn't want the park opening on time and is sabotaging the show," I suggested.

"Maybe, but how the heck are they managing all this? Apart from what seem to be administration errors, there have been things broken or tampered with. The stage that collapsed – someone deliberately destroyed those supports. There have been several attempts to get at the technical gear, but Baz is so worried that he makes sure it's guarded all day and locked away at night."

"You're kidding!" I stared at him. "I had no idea it was that bad – oh, and the theft from our hotel – was it done by the same person?"

"I suppose so," Troy said slowly. "But I can't think how it's being done. Anyway, Emma, don't you worry about it – Baz will get to the bottom of it, I'm sure. We'd better start rehearsing, hadn't we?"

"Okay." I gave myself a mental shake and tried to concentrate.

I had enough to do trying to teach Troy to ride like a warrior prince without fretting about mystery saboteurs or, more importantly, the fact that Robert probably wasn't going to speak to me ever again!

Chapter Seven

Troy had already noticed I was quieter than usual, but I could hardly tell him he was the reason Robert was ignoring me; so I let him think I was worrying about the play.

"It's going great." He tried to cheer me up and with his naturally upbeat personality he didn't fail.

Apparently the "acting bits," as Troy called them, had been rehearsed to perfection with dialogue and action combining to make the fantastic tale come to life in an exciting way.

"Now there's just the riding." Troy pulled a rueful face. "All of you are going to be awesome and the stunt guys are amazing. It's just the Sushawny prince letting you all down, and Baz is going to run out of patience with me pretty soon. He's one amazing director and I jumped at the chance to work with him, but with his reputation as a perfectionist I should have realized I was never going to get away with my poor riding."

"He thinks you're perfect for the prince," I said. "And with a bit of practice you and Crystal will be fine."

"Thanks, Em." He gave me yet another hug and I was glad no one was around to report back to Robert.

"Luckily I don't do as much riding as the rest of you because I'm busy with the acting. But Baz wants me to look dramatic and showy when I'm aboard Crystal. Considering all I've ever done is walk, trot, and canter in an indoor arena, you're going to have your work cut out, Emma!"

Having witnessed the mess he'd made of the simple scene the day before, I privately agreed and read the detailed instructions he'd brought along with a slightly sinking feeling.

"We'll try scene two," I decided. "It's a simple canter in, halt, and flying dismount. Rocco and I then lead Crystal away returning at the end of your dialogue, again at canter. This time I don't stop and you vault into Crystal's saddle as we draw level."

He gave a hollow laugh. "Nothing to it!"

The crew had marked out an area for us to work in, so we dropped behind it and put the horses into canter for the entrance. Troy and Crystal looked good together and once the make-up and costume people had added their magic, the combination of handsome blond prince and dazzling white horse would really set bells ringing for his fans. I even gave an appreciative shudder myself at the thought, despite preferring Robert's smoldering dark looks. Troy sat well, his upper body moving in rhythm with the three beats of his horse's canter and I could see how relaxed and supple he was. Although he hadn't done much riding he'd been taught properly, and when I called to him to slow in readiness for the halt I saw his outside hand give the correct take-and-give aid. Crystal came to a very creditable stop, which was completely ruined by Troy shuffling around, throwing his leg over the front of the saddle, and sliding downwards, nearly falling flat on his face.

"What was *that*?" I asked and his amazing blue eyes looked up into mine.

"My version of a flying dismount – more like the last flap of a dying duck, wasn't it?"

I wasn't sure what Baz had in mind, but thought it was probably something I'd seen the stunt riders do where they leapt, Cossack style, with their feet on the horse's back and from there did a forward or back flip through the air to the ground.

Far too ambitious for someone like Troy, I thought, and decided instead to teach him a Western-style dismount, keeping one foot in the stirrup as he swung the other leg confidently to land, sweeping grandly forward onto the stage. Not as spectacular, obviously, but it would still look pretty cool. It took several attempts but Troy worked so hard it wasn't long before he had it. Then we put it together with the extended canter and added the part where I rode past, scooped up Crystal's reins, and left the arena with both horses.

"It's still a bit rough around the edges but it's coming." I looked at Troy who was lying flat out on the grass, panting. "What's the matter with you?"

"I'm exhausted." He opened one eye and gave me his dazzling grin. "You're wearing me out, Em."

"Tough," I said hard-heartedly. "You've got to learn how to vault back on now."

He groaned theatrically and staggered to his feet. "I don't have a clue. You show me first."

I started off gently at first, with Rocco just standing, then getting him moving forward in trot while I ran beside him. With my left hand holding the reins on his neck while placing my right one over the pommel, I grasped the saddle on the far side. I pushed off with both feet, springing upwards while supporting my weight on my right arm, then swung my right leg over the saddle, being careful not to thump down hard as I landed on Rocco's back.

I then gathered up the reins, calling to Troy, "I'm now in control and ready to do whatever comes next and the whole thing has taken less than two complete strides of the pony."

"It looks impossible," Troy said flatly. "I'll never get it."

I slid off Rocco's back and smiled at him. "Yes you will. Try it with Crystal just standing first; then I'll run with you the first few times to get the timing right."

Crystal was amazingly patient and kept going forward time after time, even when Troy, gaining confidence with every try, swung his leg so strongly he flew straight over the other side. Before we stopped to give the horses a break, he'd managed several perfect vaults in a row and only groaned quietly when I said we'd be doing it in canter next. Someone came over with a message from Baz and I, for one, was extremely relieved to hear the director wouldn't be joining us as we had a long way to go before we would be perfect for him. We were to carry on practicing and he'd see what we'd achieved the following day.

"You can tell dear Baz the one thing that can be guaranteed is a good crop of bruises." Troy rubbed his skinned elbow. "But Emma's making sure I don't land on my head too often, so I'll still be able to wear my crown!"

I laughed at the pained face he was pulling. "Talking

of crowns, when do we get to try on our costumes? Judging from the scenes around the roller coaster they're amazing – I can't wait."

"You're going to look gorgeous," Troy said. "And so are you, Rocco. You get this really wild robe with scarlet flashes, Emma, while your horse has matching streamer things in his mane and tail and a jeweled bridle. The rest of the Sushawny are brightly colored while Rick and Tsar are black and silver."

"What about you?" I wanted to know.

"Oh, I'm the pretty boy prince, all white and gold – Crystal even has gold hooves to match my boots." He danced around waving his soda can in the air. "Won't we look just *lovely*?"

He really was very funny and sweet, and I enjoyed the time with him so much I nearly forgot to worry about Robert. I was determined to set things straight, to make sure Rob knew he still meant more to me than any TV star. But once again, it seemed like everything was against us. I was last to get back to the hotel and only had time for a quick shower and change before the coach arrived to take us into town. I couldn't see Robert anywhere, and as I plunked myself down on the seat next to Alice I said casually, "I hope the driver waits for the others. It's only half full."

"Not everyone wanted to go into town," Alice replied, looking slightly embarrassed. "Robert's gone out with his dad and – um – I don't know about the rest."

I was pleased Rob and his father were getting together again and tried not to worry that it meant I couldn't get to talk things through with him yet.

"That's cool. Where's Darren, I wonder?" I thought

Fox would be bound to know what his roommate was doing, but he shrugged.

"Don't ask me. The guy's a complete weirdo, always wandering off on his own. Last night he woke me up whispering on his cell phone for hours. Something about his brother being a failed actor. I felt like telling him I wished he'd do the same and give up trying to ride in this show."

I was hardly listening and stood up to peer around at the rest of the coach. "What, no Trudy? I thought she'd be bound to come. Of course if she's not here, it means no Stuart either. I wonder what they're up to?"

"Swimming." Alice still sounded reluctant and I wanted to know why.

"Well, Trudy said she'd rather wait till Robert got back at eight o'clock, than go on the coach." My friend didn't really want to tell me, I knew. "She – er – wants him to teach her how to dive."

Again I felt a hot, painful stab of jealousy and couldn't help thinking that in his present mood Robert would probably much rather splash about with Trudy than talk to me.

"That's cool too," I said, trying not to show I cared. "So, what do you both want to do tonight? I thought a burger and maybe bowling or something."

"Burger's good, but Alice wants to look at the shops. She says she's getting withdrawal symptoms," Fox teased, and I realized he was getting to like her a lot.

"Fine with me." I hoped I wasn't going to end up trailing behind them like a left shoe, and I started missing Robert even more.

We all got off the bus and were reminded to return in

70

two hours, so Troy had been right about not getting much time to do anything. It was a nice enough place; we enjoyed our food and window shopping, choosing the most expensive clothes and gadgets. We found a big mall where the stores stayed open all evening. Alice made us laugh, as in the middle of checking through the titles in a book store, she told us she'd seen someone familiar.

"Not him, is it?" Fox pointed to a giant poster of Troy's face, on display to advertise the Fantasy play. "Emma knows *him* pretty well, just ask her!"

This was a dig at me because, to their disappointment, I wouldn't talk about my day very much, partly because I didn't want them to tell Robert, and partly because I thought it would be mean of me to let all the Pony Club kids know what a novice rider Troy was.

"No," Alice replied impatiently. "Not the poster. That guy over there by the CDs."

"You mean the one in the blue cap?" I said, recognizing the lanky form immediately.

"Yeah. He looks like someone I know, only I can't think who."

"He's one of the crew, silly," I laughed. "And so is the shorter one next to him. They were both working on the seats this morning."

"Oh." Alice looked puzzled. "That's not who I was thinking of then."

"Em's right, there are three or four more crew members behind them." Fox pointed and Alice screwed up her eyes to look.

"Oh yeah, you're right. Funny, though."

We didn't ask why it was so odd, having suddenly realized we only had ten minutes to get back to the bus. We

71

had to sprint to make it and were the last to arrive. We were soon on our way back to Adventure World and our hotel.

"We'll probably be told to go straight to bed for an early night again," Fox said gloomily. "In fact, it wouldn't surprise me if the kids that stayed are already tucked in and fast asleep."

But he was wrong. The big room with the Play Station and music system was still humming with activity. Everyone was hunting around, moving tables and sofas and peering under cushions.

"What have you lost?" Alice asked.

Darren looked up briefly "Trudy's necklace. She took it off to swim and left it in this room, but it's gone."

"It's probably in the changing room or somewhere," Alice began in a bored voice, but Trudy, shouted irritably across the room, "I heard that, Alice! It most certainly is *not*! I deliberately put it on this table so I wouldn't lose it at the swimming pool. You could at least help look – it's extremely valuable."

"You should have put it in the safe then," Alice muttered and I couldn't help grinning, till I saw Trudy was practically in tears.

Reluctantly I asked, "Where haven't you looked?"

"We've tried everywhere." Trudy was quite panicky. "I think it must have been stolen!"

A shocked murmur rumbled through our group.

"You mean like before?" Ginny was really concerned. "That means it *must* be someone inside the hotel."

"Well it doesn't take a genius to work that out, does it?" Trudy flounced away and I glanced quickly at Robert to see how he was reacting.

He seemed almost disinterested as he sat flicking through a magazine, and I felt a stab of anger that he could act so cool and not even bother to say hello. If he was still mad because of Troy's greeting, he could just loosen up and get over it.

All the kids who'd been into town on the bus spent ages searching for Trudy's necklace. We were probably only looking in all the places that had been searched before, but I think everyone wanted it found, not particularly for Trudy's sake, but to prove there was no connection with the earlier thefts. Some security men turned up and one of them spoke to Trudy and wrote down all the details of the disappearance. She was very weepy and dramatic by now and Alice, who was crawling around the floor nearby, heard everything she said. When we eventually went off for our delayed early night she told me all about it.

"Apparently Trudy made a big deal of leaving the necklace on the table, saying very loudly she was putting it there for safe keeping, so everyone in the room would have known about it. The security guys say no one else went in there, not even hotel staff, so it must have been one of the other kids. Trudy threw a real fit when they said that and started bawling that we all hated her and it was done out of spite."

I groaned. "What did they say to that?"

"They all looked a bit alarmed, but I think they'd figured out what a drama queen she is. They told her if it's been stolen it's because it's gold and valuable."

"I suppose they took all the names of the kids who stayed here this evening and will probably question them. Except for Robert, I guess, since he was with her in the swimming pool when it went missing."

"No," Alice said slowly. "He wasn't. He came back early and in a bad mood and said he didn't feel like giving a diving lesson. Trudy thumped the necklace down in front of him and said he could make himself useful by guarding that instead."

I stared at her. "It gets worse by the minute. How does Robert explain the disappearance if he was supposed to be watching the thing?"

Alice didn't look at me. "He's still in such a foul mood he hasn't bothered to say. I tried talking to him about it, but he just shrugged and said he didn't notice it had gone missing until Trudy started making a scene. Then he stomped off before the security guys could talk to him, which isn't the cleverest thing he could have done."

She was right about that, and I felt my heart sinking at the thought that if Robert didn't snap out of his black mood he might find himself the chief suspect in this and all the previous thefts!

Chapter Eight

My mom always says that if I've got a problem to get a good night's sleep and it'll look much better in the morning. All I can say, Mom, is – WRONG! After my usual tussle getting Alice out of her bed, I pattered swiftly down to breakfast bent on having a quiet, calm word with Robert about his attitude and the potential minefield he was creating for himself. I was pretty sure he'd be resentful and difficult but was determined to make him listen. I felt thoroughly deflated to see an empty chair where he should be. Trudy was at the table, unsmiling and looking sulky.

"Any news of your necklace?" I just wanted it found but she shook her head glumly.

"Nope."

"I'm sorry." I was being genuine; she was a pain and I couldn't stand her, but she didn't deserve this.

"It's okay, Emma," the ever-present Stuart said pointedly. "We know it wasn't *you* who stole it."

I took this to be a dig at Robert and said furiously "Grow up, Stuart. It wasn't *any* of us."

"Well, Robert's finally gone to talk to Security." Stuart was still sneering. "Isn't that big of him?"

I ignored him and glanced at my watch, realizing I wasn't going to have my chat with Rob before work began for the day. We were being taken to Wardrobe before rehearsal, we'd been told. We all filed out and onto the coach again. Robert was the last one to board and chose a seat as far away from me as he possibly could. In fact he sat completely alone, hunched into a corner talking to no one, staring mutinously out of the window. The Wardrobe department had been set up in a big trailer at the rear of the stage. It would double as a dressing room for the actors to save traveling back and forth. We soon arrived and piled off the coach, eager to get our first sight of the costumes.

"Uh-oh – look." Fox pointed to a grim-looking knot of security men, clustered around the trailer door. "What's going on now?"

Ginny, who was ahead of us, turned around and hissed "More trouble! Someone tried to set fire to the trailer last night. Luckily some of the crew spotted smoke and put it out before any damage was done to the costumes."

Now that we were closer, we could see a scorched, blackened mat thrown out onto the ground and there were smoke trails on the inside of the open door. Everyone started talking at once, but we all fell quiet as Baz's jeep arrived and he climbed out. For the first time he wasn't bouncing; all the energy seemed sapped out of him, and his tired eyes had dark, pouchy circles under them. He said a brief "good morning" to us all then disappeared into the trailer. He wasn't long, and as soon as he left one of the staff came out with a printed sheet and started calling out our names in groups of four. Although I was still worrying about Robert and feeling sorry for Baz and all his problems, I couldn't help enjoying the costume fitting. We knew what to expect from the computer pictures of the story we'd seen in Fantasy Land, but it was fun actually putting on the beautiful garments Baz and his team had come up with. Although fitting was necessary in that the costumes varied in size and length, they were loose and roomy so they could be slipped over our ordinary clothes, which made things much easier. The trousers were great, sort of slashed and gathered with colored trailing parts that would stream out dramatically when we rode into the arena. The tunic tops were similar and there were pointed fabric slipovers to hide our boots, and horned skull caps made of glittery netting that were to be fitted over our riding hats, hiding them completely. Once the staff were satisfied we looked okay, each complete costume was bagged up, marked with our name, and hung on long rails ready for wear on dress-rehearsal day. As usual it was all done very efficiently and professionally so it wasn't long before we were all outfitted and back on the coach to fetch our ponies.

Rocco gave me a pleased whicker of greeting and I hugged him tight before starting to get him ready for the day's rehearsal. He'd rolled as he always did, but it didn't take long to brush his coat back to gleaming ebony. While I groomed I told him all about the lovely braids and bridle decorations neatly packaged ready for him and the other ponies.

"While you're talking, ask him if he's got any ideas about Trudy's necklace and the fire last night." Alice already had Paint tacked up and they came over to join us. "You're always saying how clever your horse is, so maybe he'll have some ideas."

I carefully straightened Rocco's numnah before putting on his saddle and frowned at her. "You're not saying the fire and the theft are connected, are you?"

"Unless Adventure World is dripping with criminals, I'd say it was the same person, yeah."

"But – " I couldn't work it out. "I can see how the costumes getting destroyed would ruin the play's progress, but the thefts are different, surely."

"They probably are – the security guys think one of us is doing it just to get the money, but it could cause a massive disruption if everyone gets fed up with losing things and decides to go home."

She was right, and I remembered it being one of my earlier concerns.

"There could have been someone, an outsider, prowling around last night." I tried to think of an explanation that didn't involve any of us kids (especially Robert). "They could have climbed through a window at the hotel maybe, waited till everyone had gone to sleep, and then gone to the arena to start the fire. It's not that far to walk, only twenty minutes or so."

"They're saying the fire was probably started *before* the necklace was taken." Alice was tightening Paint's girth. "A screwed up length of paper was shoved through the mail slot and ignited, but it just smoldered before some of the crew, that group we saw in town actually, drove back in their van and decided to check out the arena. It was lucky they did, and from now on security's going to be increased, so there will be a patrol every night."

"That still means someone could have started the fire, though they sound pretty amateurish, and then gone to

79

the hotel and stolen Trudy's necklace," I insisted, and she gave me a funny look.

"Well yeah, but it isn't going to be a complete stranger, is it? Practically anyone who didn't go into town could have left the hotel for a while and no one would have questioned it. After all, Robert – " she stopped abruptly.

"You were going to say Robert was out in the park *and* in the room where the theft happened, weren't you?" I was mad at her.

"His name's bound to crop up when everyone's talking about this, and he's not helping by being so moody and quiet. Can't you get through to him, Emma?"

"I wish I could." I swung into Rocco's saddle. "I'll try again at break. Come on, everyone else is on their way."

The arena, with its completed seating, was now set for us to rehearse, and with Baz in full command we were soon so involved I had to put aside the nagging worry about Robert and get to work. The riding was fantastic and Rocco and I had the greatest time galloping and jumping across, through, and over the wonderful Fantasy staging in the arena. We were still divided into our opposing tribes of course, and our group was delighted to find the Sushawny made more entrances and did more spectacular riding than the invading Zardonnes.

Rick and Tsar led us in each time, and Rick's imaginative displays were excellent and quite challenging. Baz was in charge of fine-tuning each approach we made, and with his great eye for detail, he was beginning to produce some truly stunning effects. My favorite part was at the end of the first act in the middle of the play (we still hadn't run it through from start to finish) when the Sushawny are called upon by their prince to parade a show of strength to the elder members of the tribe. Troy would be standing at center stage, dressed in his amazing white and gold apparel, the lights glittering on the jeweled crown he wore, as he flung his hand skywards to signal his warriors' entrance. On this cue, trumpets sounded, drums rolled, and a great roar echoed round the arena as the Sushawny appeared. Rick, clothed in black and silver, came in first at gallop, one foot on Tsar's saddle, the other on Crystal's as he stood astride the two horses, one black and silver, the other white and gold. He drove them in a curve in front of the audience, then back toward the stage. The other stunt riders followed, double vaulting, performing headstands and "death hangs" in their saddles, all at full speed. Then came Rocco and I, leading the rest of the colorful tribe. We galloped and swooped in intricate circles and serpentines between the trees and boulders on the edge of the arena. Then at last we were uniting, forming ranks to join in military precision at the central point between stage and audience. We raised our swords as one and moved to stand behind our prince. His own gleaming sword held aloft in a two-handed salute, Troy shouted *"The Sushawny!"* and a great cheer with bells, trumpets, drums, and flashing lights swelled into a mighty crescendo before a complete black-out and (hopefully) deafening applause.

Not bad, eh? Of course it didn't look exactly like that the first time we did it, or even the twenty-first to be honest, but with a bit of imagination you could tell from the start it was going to be magnificent. I hadn't actually realized how much imagination was required when it came to rehearsing a play. For a start no one is dressed or made up. We were all just ordinary-looking people belting around on horses. In the initial stages, there were no actors on stage or any lights and music; someone just shouted the cue line and off we went. I couldn't wait to see Troy actually up there being the prince, and was unwise enough to say so to Alice, not realizing Trudy was standing within earshot. She immediately ran over and whispered to Robert and I saw him turn away and shrug as if he didn't care.

Alice told me not to worry about it. "She's a total cat, that girl. Last night she told Robert off because he didn't guard her stupid necklace, but today she's still trying to come between you and him!"

I tried hard to follow Alice's advice and not care, but I could feel my jealousy knotting and twisting inside. We sat down on the grass together to watch the Zardonnes rehearse their first entrance. It wasn't as colorful as ours, Baz wanted the cheers to be for the Sushawny, but the riding action was still fast and furious. The tribe came into the arena from the opposite side to us, and were led through the spooky trees and rocks to the same central point. Robert, as one of the tallest, was at the back and was to make the most sweeping curve, galloping Juniper straight at the audience, then veering away at the very last moment. I'd seen him make the entrance before, and admired the smooth rhythm and control of the aggressive movement he'd been set to do.

This time, however, something went horribly wrong. As Juniper landed from a perfect flying leg change, the gray horse slipped and went crashing to the ground,

spilling Robert from the saddle. Juniper was on his feet immediately and cantered away only to be caught by Rick. To my absolute horror Robert didn't move at all, not a muscle nor a hair. He just lay there in a crumpled, motionless, utterly frightening huddle.

Chapter Nine

The response was immediate. Two First-Aiders raced to Robert's side and to my extreme relief, I saw him move and try to sit up. They seemed to want him to lie still until they'd checked him over, and one carefully removed his hard hat to look at the side of his head. Meanwhile someone else was inspecting the ground, head bowed, walking slowly across the grass where Juniper had slipped. Somehow I wasn't surprised when he stopped and bent to look at something, then called to Baz in an urgent voice.

Baz had been hovering near Robert, but he hurried over to peer down at the ground and I saw his worried expression become even graver. Of course, I wanted to run to Robert and hear him say he was fine, but the stupid knot of jealousy and uncertainty I was feeling held me back. After what seemed like ages he was helped to his feet and a paramedic started walking with him toward a car that had pulled up to the edge of the arena.

"He's badly hurt! They're taking him to a doctor!" I clutched Alice's arm and she patted my hand reassuringly.

"They're just going to get him checked out, that's all."

I didn't know what to do with myself. I was so upset and felt helpless and useless and worried all at the same time. The only practical thing I could think of was to make sure Robert's horse was okay so, leaving Rocco with Alice, I ran over to where Rick was still calming the gray pony.

"Is he all right?" I asked breathlessly. "Juniper, I mean."

"He's fine. Not a scratch on him." The short, stocky man looked at me with concern. "You don't look too good though, Emma. You're as white as a sheet."

"Robert's a – a friend." I said. "It was horrible seeing him hurt in an accident like that."

"Even worse if it wasn't really an accident," Rick said slowly. "Look, Emma, you'll probably feel better if you *do* something for your friend. You'll only be in the way of the paramedic guys, so how about taking his pony to turn out in the paddock? Having the rest of the day off will be the best thing for him."

"Okay." I took Juniper's reins willingly. "I'll walk him back slowly."

"Good girl." He glanced sharply behind me where Baz and some of the others were pacing around the big three-tiered stage. "I'd better go and see what's happening over there."

I clicked my tongue and Juniper followed me at once, looking, as Rick had said, completely fine. It would have been all right to ride him back to the paddock, but the gentle walk would give him a chance to stretch out any stiffness he was feeling after his fall. I explained what I was doing to Alice and she suggested I ride Rocco so that Juniper would have his friend to keep him company.

86

"We'll all be back for the horses' lunch break soon," she pointed out. "Or I can come with you now if you like."

"No, you stay so you can find out where they've taken Robert and what's going to be happening for the rest of the day. Rick seemed to think there's more trouble."

She looked over to where the group of men stood in deep discussion on the stage and nodded. It was almost spooky, riding quietly through the empty fields with only Rocco and Juniper for company. They'd spent lots of time together, of course, but I'd always had Robert at my side talking and laughing with me. I missed him badly and wondered if we'd ever regain the wonderful closeness we had shared. I gave Juniper extra tidbits when I released the two ponies into their paddock, and Rocco rubbed his black nose affectionately on my arm as if to say he understood. The two of them trotted across the grass together and went to their favorite spot to roll and squirm ecstatically. I sat on the fence and watched them both, and although their antics made me smile, I couldn't shake off the underlying feeling of loneliness that had haunted me all day. Alice, when she and Fox arrived with Paint and Gabby, didn't make things any better.

"Robert's been taken to the hospital," she announced, adding swiftly when she saw the alarm in my face, "Just for observation – it's standard when someone's knocked out, apparently. Oh, and that cat Trudy invited herself along! She just got into the car with him – Stuart's going nuts about it."

"I – I hope Robert's okay," was all I managed to stammer, wishing passionately that it was me who was with him now.

"He'll be all right," Fox said confidently. "They're probably being extra specially careful because it wasn't an accident."

I'd been trying not to consider that. "But his horse slipped and he fell. Surely it's as simple as that."

"But the reason Juniper slipped was that someone, our old friend the arsonist and thief presumably, had been slopping oily stuff around," Alice said. "They found two or three patches on the stage and several more spilled in the arena. It's amazing more horses weren't sent crashing and doubly lucky that Robert and Juniper weren't badly hurt."

"This is turning into a nightmare." I slipped off the fence and opened the gate for them to bring their ponies through. "What did Baz say about it?"

"He's badly shaken. He must realize how terrible it could have been, especially if one of his star actors had slipped and hurt himself." Fox took Gabby's head collar off and gave her a pat. "He seemed to be on the point of calling the whole show off."

"Oh no!" Despite all the problems I really wanted the Fantasy play to go ahead. "But they've put so much work into it, they can't abandon it now."

"Baz feels the same, but like I said, he's totally rattled. He told all of us to be on our guard the whole time now. Extra security is coming in but we're to look for anything even remotely suspicious and report it at once."

"What about the rest of today?" If we aren't rehearsing I could try to get a lift to the hospital and see Robert.

"Schedule's changed – we're to practice sword fighting this afternoon – in the field, not the arena."

I thought that was all right, better than just hanging

around worrying, and once we got involved it was really interesting. The moves were quite tightly choreographed and I was pleased to see Ginny was making notes for Robert, though I spitefully hoped no one was doing the same for Trudy. Alice, of course, had seen how upset I was and tried to cheer me up by saying it had been all Trudy's idea to get in the hospital car.

"Robert will be driven crazy by her fussing over him, though she'll probably spend half her time making eyes at any young doctors who go by."

I hoped she was right, but I was so angry I just couldn't talk about it. "What about Alan? Has anyone told him about Rob's fall?"

"Robert's dad, you mean?" Fox stopped twirling his fake sword around his head for a minute. "Yeah, Ginny said he's gone rushing off to the hospital to be with Rob even though he's still up to his eyes in work over at Space World."

"I think Alan's a really great dad. I can't understand why Robert's got such a downer about him." Alice cautiously tried a swirl with her own sword. "You ought to have a word with him, Emma."

I tried a double swirl, but my heart wasn't in it. "I've tried; he won't listen, especially to me."

"Talk to Alan then." Alice clambered back into Paint's saddle. "Come on, break's over. We've got lots more fighting to do!"

It was an energetic afternoon and by the time I'd settled Rocco for the night, checked on Juniper again, and had my shower, it was time for our evening meal. There was still no sign of Robert or Trudy. Stuart was sitting at the table glowering sulkily and he spent the next hour loitering in the reception hall waiting for Trudy's return. I was just walking through when someone called him into the games room. The moment he left, the doors opened and in came Alan. He looked weary and very harassed, and when I saw Robert behind his father, his face dark and moody, I understood why. Trudy was there too, of course, chattering endlessly as usual. I hesitated before stopping to turn toward them.

"Hi, Rob. Are you okay?" I could hear the stilted tone of my voice and wasn't really surprised when Robert merely grunted and walked straight past me.

"I'll see you in the morning – " Alan broke off as his son just kept going and I felt a rush of anger at Robert for treating us both so badly. Trudy flashed her insincere smile and trotted puppy-like after him. I was gripping the stair rail so tightly my knuckles were white. Alan seemed to notice, and his eyes were sympathetic.

"Sorry, Emma. Rob really shouldn't take his bad temper out on you."

"Or you." I felt sad for both of us. "Why is he being like this?"

Alan sighed and sat down on a sofa. "Today's fall hasn't helped, of course, but before that I was beginning to think it had been a really dumb idea to bring Robert here. He seems to be testing me all the time."

"Testing you?"

"Yes, he's suspicious of my motives. He says I ignored him for months, which isn't true. I was just working such long hours, and now he says I've brought him here and dumped him with a bunch of people he doesn't like."

"He's fallen out with me too, but I guess you knew that."

"So I gather. He hasn't given any details, but says you're the same as me, too quick to ditch him when something better shows up."

"That is so unfair!" I felt like following Robert and bashing him on his sore head. "I'd never dump him for anyone."

"I'm sure he knows that deep down, but the split between his mom and me seems to have hit him much harder than I realized. He doesn't trust *anyone* any more." Poor Alan rubbed his tired eyes. "Try not to worry about it, Emma, I'm sure Robert will realize we're there for him eventually. I'd better go – I have to start work very early to make up for lost time, then leave when the shops open in town so I can get Robert a new hat."

"New hat?" I repeated stupidly.

"Yeah, they've just told me his hard hat got dented in the fall today. Luckily his head didn't. Baz won't allow him to ride wearing an unsafe hat, so I have to bring him a new one as soon as I can tomorrow morning,"

"Oh well, it means Rob can sleep in," I said, thinking Alan looked as if he should do the same.

He smiled wanly and left, leaving me unsure whether to go and yell a few home truths at Robert or give him a big hug and tell him everything was going to be all right. In the end I did neither but if I'd gone for the hug option I'd have been very, very wrong. Things did *not* turn out okay. In fact, as far as Robert was concerned, they got a hundred million times worse!

Chapter Ten

I woke up the next morning with that horrible sinking feeling you get when something's wrong. I can't pretend I was being psychic and seeing into the future or anything. The dull ache was caused by my unhappiness at the way things were between Robert and me and the frustration of not being able to fix them. He hadn't spoken to me at all the night before, completely ignoring me every time I looked his way. Trudy had remained firmly glued to his side the whole time so there was no way I could try talking to him. He wasn't at breakfast and Trudy didn't help my mood by loudly informing everyone that she'd been in to see him and he looked so sweet when he was asleep.

"He probably knew she was there and was faking it," Alice whispered. "Personally, I'd pretend I was dead if she came into my room."

I agreed completely but couldn't help thinking that Robert probably liked all the attention he was getting from Trudy. Still, there was too much to do to spend the day moping. I set off with the others, determined to concentrate on the rehearsal and put Robert out of my mind. Once we were all tacked up and ready, a buzz of excitement surged through our crowd when we heard we'd be running through a couple of scenes in the arena with, for the first time, the actors doing their parts. We rode up through the fields together, then separated into our tribes. When I heard a few girly squeals I knew Troy had arrived to join us.

"Hi, everyone!" His friendly voice carried clearly. "I hear your riding's going great. I just hope I don't let you all down."

I watched him bring Crystal to the front of the Sushawny tribe and thought, quite proudly, that even without the crown and makeup, he looked every inch a prince.

"Hello, Em." He leaned forward and gave me his usual greeting kiss and I heard a sort of concentrated "whoosh" as every girl present drew in her breath.

The scene we were to rehearse started with a relatively simple entrance with Troy cantering in a casual, almost insolent way to meet his father the king for the first time in the play. The Sushawny tribe, not yet in warrior mode, followed their prince as happy, fun-loving supporters. Troy and Crystal entered from the left and we spread out behind them to form a curved frame around the arena where they cantered in a wide circle before approaching the stage. They then did a turn on the forehand (I'd shown Troy how) to face the audience. Then the prince raised his arm and pointed to a rider on either side of the arena, a signal for them to gallop in front of him, crossing diagonally, their ponies almost touching as the tribe whooped and cheered.

We'd practiced this entrance in the field, without Troy or setting, and it had gone really well. I suppose what with having a well-known TV star present, plus other actors *and* all the crew, some stage fright from the Pony Club kids was inevitable. Our first few attempts that morning were frankly dismal. Alice was one of the first riders to go and she said later that being pointed at by Troy Mitchell was just too much for a girl to take! She not only got the timing completely wrong, but she forgot to stop and simply carried on galloping till she and Paint disappeared back out of the arena. Baz was bouncing up and down and yelling so much I thought he'd burst. Gradually everyone calmed down and worked hard till the entrance was perfect.

"I liked that," Baz announced as we lolled about recovering. "In fact I think we'll use the same format for the Zardonnes' first scene. Mirroring the image will double the effect for the audience."

The Zardonnes, who'd laughed a lot at our mistakes, looked horrified at the thought, and we Sushawny settled happily down to watch them and get our own back. You'd have thought Trudy had never done a Pony Club game in her life, the way she carried on and made Baz repeat the instructions ten times. On their first attempt she aimed Giselle in completely the wrong direction and when she finally did get it right she didn't whoop or cheer – she burst into embarrassing loud tears. I could see Baz getting more and more uptight but after a bit of patient coaching from Jim, she finally got it right, and the fast moving crisscross riding began to look really good.

It was now nearly coffee break time and just as I was wondering where Robert and his new hat were, disaster struck. Three pairs of riders had changed places, galloping their diagonal lines, crossing perfectly and making tight, neat turns as they brought their horses to halt. The fourth pair was comprised of Darren on Socks, and another tall kid called Jake, riding a solid-looking bay. They both set off at precisely the same time and galloped vigorously toward the crossing point in the center and looking perfect, until Socks inexplicably swerved, veering off his line into the path of the fast-approaching bay horse. Jake did his best to avoid the chestnut pony, but it was impossible and the shoulder of the bay caught Socks a glancing blow. The impact sent Darren hurtling from his saddle to crash heavily on the ground where he immediately rolled over, grabbing his leg and howling in pain.

Again paramedics rushed in, a stunt rider caught the fleeing Socks, and Baz called everyone to dismount and stay calm. Jake slid off his pony's back immediately, looking sick and shaken and I saw Robert appear suddenly and run to him. He took the bay horse's reins and checked him over, while talking in quiet tones to calm Jake, who was obviously in shock. This was more like the caring, dependable Robert I'd always known and I wished I could tell him so, but this wasn't the time. Rehearsal was, of course, suspended and before we even left the arena Baz and his assistants were hunting around at the point where Socks had swerved, bending to peer at every blade of grass with fierce concentration.

"Are they looking for another booby trap?" I asked, but Fox shook his head.

"I don't see how it could be. We've been riding around the arena half the morning and it seemed perfect. I think the accident was just that – an accident – partly caused by Darren's awful riding."

"Poor old Darren, you never have a good word for him." Alice thumped his arm.

"You don't have to share a room with him," Fox said darkly. "The guy's weird, and as for being a Pony Club team member, well it's hard to believe."

"He *is* a terrible rider," I agreed, having always thought that even Troy was better than Darren.

"So is Trudy, come to that." Alice couldn't resist a dig at her. "But even if you're right and the crash wasn't caused deliberately, it puts the play in jeopardy again."

"I know. Baz must be at the end of his tether by now, and I wouldn't be surprised if we all get told to pack up and go home."

"Nah, Baz will get this play up and running if it's the last thing he does," Fox said. "Darren wasn't badly hurt anyway; he was just making a big deal out of falling off."

I hoped he was right and I also hoped the enforced break would give me a chance to talk to Robert. Juniper was already back in his paddock so, thinking Rob must have returned to the hotel, I suggested we go back there too.

"Good idea," Alice said agreeably. "I'd like a swim, how about you two?"

"You and Fox go," I said quickly. "I – um – want to see someone first."

"Don't know why you bother." Alice knew who I meant. "He's turned into a total loser if you ask me, all moody and miserable."

Fox looked at us both. "Who has?"

"No one." I walked ahead, feeling cross.

Alice had never been as close to Robert as I had, but I thought she was being unfairly harsh. I was determined to tell him I still felt the same as ever and hoped he'd be in some quiet corner of the hotel so we could really talk. When we got there we found there *were* no quiet corners. Most of the kids had come back and there were angry little knots of them standing around the games room, arms folded and voices raised.

"What's going on?" I grabbed Ginny's arm as she went by.

"More trouble," she said. "Stuart and his room mate found their room ransacked when they got back just now."

"Oh no!" Alice groaned. "Still, everyone's stuff is in the safe so they haven't had anything taken, have they?"

"Afraid so. Stuart's aunt sent him some spending money yesterday and he forgot to hand it in." Ginny looked worried. "The trouble is, if it's one of us kids like everybody says, then it can only be one person this time."

"What do you mean?" I was almost too scared to ask.

"From the time Stuart left his room after breakfast we were all at rehearsal. All you Sushawny were present and we Zardonnes were just one short, not counting Darren who got carted off to the hospital after his fall."

"You're talking about Robert, aren't you?" I said it louder than I meant and several heads turned to look at me. "He was here waiting for his dad to bring a new hard hat and there's no way he'd have gone near Stuart's room. No *WAY!*"

"You know, Emma I really hope you're right." Stuart was standing right behind me. "Because I'd hate to think Robert is the one who's causing all this grief. Not only my money, but the other guys' earlier this week, and poor Trudy just the other night."

97

"It – it wouldn't be Robert who stole from me, would it?" Trudy was in floods of tears again.

"I hope it wasn't him." Stuart sounded very sincere. "Anyway he wouldn't know to go looking in my room for money. I mean – he didn't know there was any in there."

"Oh Stuart!" Trudy looked at him with wet, teary eyes. "He did know you'd been sent some cash; we both heard you talking about it last night."

"And he could have known I was running too late to put it in the safe today." Stuart looked as if the thought had just struck him. "His room's right down the corridor from ours – he could have heard me leaving."

I looked around at everyone in despair. They all thought Robert was guilty, Robert who I'd known for years and would trust with absolutely anything I owned. The need to speak to him was just too great and I turned and ran upstairs, heading for his room on the floor above mine. Every door in the corridor was closed and my footsteps echoed faintly as I approached Robert's room. Taking a deep breath I knocked briskly and waited for him to answer. There was no sound from inside though I strained my ears for any sign of movement. I tapped once more, then opened the door and looked in. Robert was sitting on one of the beds, his knees hunched up under his chin, his expression sullen.

"You *are* here," I said, a bit stupidly. "Didn't you hear me knock?"

"Yes." He gave me a hard, blank look. "But I thought if I didn't answer you'd take the hint and shove off."

"Oh for heaven's sake, Rob." I couldn't believe how stupid he was being. "Don't you think you're in enough trouble?"

"What's that supposed to mean?" he sounded as though he couldn't care less, so I thought I'd try shocking him back to reality.

"It means everyone in the place except me thinks you're a thief."

His cold, fixed gaze didn't waver. "Who cares?"

"I do, for one. You've never stolen a thing in your life, so don't you think you should be convincing everyone that there's no way you'd start by ripping off your friends?"

"I don't have any friends." His voice was flat, sounding almost bored. "So if someone else in this dump has lost something, I couldn't give a darn."

Sighing with frustration I spelled out what had happened to Stuart and how Trudy had told everyone Robert knew about the money being in his room.

He shrugged. "So now Trudy's joined the ranks of people who dump me. I've got a dad who only brought me here to score points off my mom, and a so-called girlfriend who couldn't wait to ditch me for a second rate TV star. Why should I care if the blonde bimbo's also decided I'm not worth wasting time on?"

"Stop feeling sorry for yourself and get a life!" I said furiously. "Your dad wants you around and he tied himself in knots trying to get off work and see you, and I – I still like you better than a million actors even though you're being a total idiot!"

For a moment the icy stare wavered and a hopeful gleam warmed his dark eyes. "Yeah? I've heard you're crazy about Troy and I know you spend all your time with him."

"The first thing's garbage and I only help Troy with his riding so the play won't suffer."

99

"So he's not – " he hesitated, looking suddenly vulnerable. "Your boyfriend?"

"No way!" I replied with fervor and he smiled for the first time in days. "Come on downstairs, Rob. I really think you should talk to Stuart and the others, so they understand it's not you doing the stealing."

"If you want." He was still unsure and I held out my hand to hold his.

"I do want."

We walked down the sweeping Gothic staircase, ready to face the other kids together, but just as we reached the reception hall the doors burst open and in raced Troy.

"I'm looking for Emma," he called to the security guard. "Have you seen – oh there you are!"

Robert immediately stepped back and stood watching warily as Troy took my arm and walked me a few steps away.

"I'm really sorry to ask, Em." He spoke softly with his mouth close to my ear. "But could you give me and Crystal an hour this afternoon? I still can't get scene three right."

"Sure," I said quickly, just wanting him to go away so I could support Robert, but I should have known Troy and his exuberance by now.

"You're a gem, Em!" he laughed uproariously, picked me up, twirled me round and, of course, planted a kiss on my cheek. "See you later!"

He left the hotel and I didn't have to turn around to know that Robert had disappeared too, and I also knew I hadn't a chance in hell of getting him to come back.

100

Chapter Eleven

For a minute or two I just stood where I was, feeling utterly defeated. Robert had, under Trudy's malicious guidance I was sure, convinced himself that Troy and I were an item, and now that he'd seen what looked like a display of boyfriend-type affection and the arranging of a "date" he was probably convinced I'd lied when I said the actor meant nothing to me.

"What's up, Emma?" Alice came into reception to look for me. "Come for that swim, why don't you?"

"No thanks, Ali, I'm really not in the mood. I'll just meet up with you at rehearsal."

"We're back in the field after lunch aren't we?" She narrowed her eyes to peer at me. "You look upset; has Robert been giving you a hard time?"

"Yeah." I didn't tell her about him suspecting Troy was my boyfriend in case she burst out laughing. "I wanted him to come down and talk to Stuart and the others, but he won't."

"I don't think it would make any difference," Alice said candidly. "Now that Trudy thinks Robert stole her precious necklace, she's gone from being his lovesick follower to hating his guts, and she's telling everyone so."

"I don't see how anyone could think Robert is a thief," I protested. "He's totally honest, you know that."

"Well, yeah." She looked uncomfortable. "The thing is, Trudy knows how he feels about his dad and she's telling everyone Robert's stealing and creating trouble so the play will be cancelled."

"Ridiculous!" I interrupted angrily. "What would be the point?"

"Trudy thinks it would make Adventure World mad at Alan and they'd fire him." Alice saw my expression and added quickly, "I know she's an airhead and it doesn't sound very likely, but given Robert was definitely the only kid who had the opportunity to ransack Stuart's room, people are kind of taking it seriously."

I shook my head and muttered a very rude word.

"I know, I know – it's circumstantial evidence, but the more she goes on, the worse it looks. Stuart even said it was possible Robert caused Socks to swerve today because he and Juniper arrived at the arena just about the time Darren had his accident."

"Oh, *come on!*" I exploded. "You know how much Robert loves horses – he'd never try to cause a collision like that! And what about his own fall? Trudy was all over him when that happened, so how does she explain it?"

Alice shuffled her feet. "Maybe he faked it."

"Faked it! Are you completely nuts?"

"It could have been partly so he wouldn't be a suspect and also to set things up so he'd be alone in the hotel this morning." She held up her hand to stop me yelling. "I'm only telling you what's being said, Emma."

"But you think there might be something in it!" I was bitterly disappointed in her.

"I'd feel a lot better if Robert would at least talk," she said bluntly. "You've got to admit it looks strange the way he doesn't defend himself. He didn't used to be like this."

"He's only like *this* because he thinks he's been let down by his dad and his – friends."

"You included?" she shook her head. "You've always stood up for him, Em and I honestly don't know why you bother."

"I *bother* because I know the real Robert. The way he's acting now isn't him at all – something or some*one* has made him feel like this, but I'm not giving up on him."

She shrugged and I watched her go off for her swim with Fox. If we were going to rehearse later and I was to help Troy, I knew I ought to get something to eat. Squaring my shoulders, I walked into the dining room. As usual a varied buffet with a big salad bar had been set out for lunch so I put a few things on a plate and wandered over to join Ginny. She and her friends had obviously been talking about Robert because they immediately fell silent when I arrived.

"Don't mind me," I said, quite aggressively. "Or would you rather I sat somewhere else so you can carry on gossiping?"

"Of course not," Ginny said at once. "Um – was that Troy I saw with you just now?"

I felt myself going red. "He just wanted to arrange an extra rehearsal."

"You lucky thing," one of the other girls said dreamily. "He's even better in real life than on the screen. And he's a good rider too."

104

I started on my salad without enthusiasm.

"So how come you two keep putting in all this extra time together?" Ginny's eyes were twinkling and although I knew she was only teasing, I wished she'd shut up.

"It's just to get it perfect so Baz will be satisfied," I said shortly. "You know what he's like."

"Do I!" she made a grimace. "I nearly died when he said we had to do that crisscross routine. I know it's basically simple stuff but you haven't got Trudy and Darren in your tribe!"

I was glad I'd changed the subject and hoped they'd all think about the riding rather than the likelihood of Robert being guilty, or whether Troy Mitchell with his hugs and kisses was, in fact, my boyfriend. Our rehearsal back in the field went surprisingly well, but I couldn't help noticing Juniper wasn't performing at his best. Looking at Robert's tense, rigid form I understood why the gray pony was finding it difficult, having always been used to his rider's relaxed technique. After we'd finished for the day I carefully rubbed my lovely black boy down and turned him back out into his paddock, knowing the practice with Troy only involved Crystal. Rocco trotted across the grass, then stopped and whinnied, calling, I'm sure for his friend Juniper. There was no sign of Robert though, and I must admit I felt quite relieved that he wasn't around to see me set off to meet Troy. I'd just come out of the gate, chatting away to Ginny and Alice, when I saw a flash of gleaming white and realized Troy and Crystal were heading toward us.

"Ooh," Ginny said in delight. "Here comes your knight in shining armor, Emma!"

105

Troy was cantering easily and again I felt a flash of pride at how much his confidence had improved.

"Hi, Em," he called. "I thought I'd give you a lift. Hop aboard."

It would have been mean-minded of me to refuse and after all, he had no idea of the havoc he was causing in my life. As he drew alongside I obligingly vaulted up behind him and we cantered across the field, leaving envious Ginny and Alice behind. The arena was quiet, with just a couple of crewmembers fiddling around at the back of the stage and a tense-looking security guy patrolling up and down.

"Can we go through the scene five entrance where I ride Crystal onto the first level and along the front and down again?" Troy asked. "Rick will be rehearsing Tsar on the stage later, so I need to practice this one before he gets here."

"Okay." I paced out the distance and showed him where to bring Crystal to a halt, then stood on the stage to watch.

Troy wheeled the gray to take her behind the stage and begin his entrance. I looked around idly while I waited for his return. The high, undulating platform at the back of the stage above level four was being modified to make it more closely resemble the roller coaster, with two of the crew busily hammering and sawing. One of them was the tall, skinny guy we'd seen in town and I wondered absently just who it was he'd reminded Alice of. As he was now kneeling, his face half obscured by the blue cap he wore, I couldn't see him clearly and soon forgot him as Troy and Crystal thundered toward me. Their halt was tidy and efficient, but Troy had overshot the mark so poor Crystal had to make an awkward half pace when stepping up to the first level of the stage. It looked messy and I knew it wouldn't pass Baz's scrutiny so I made Troy do the whole thing again several times until he was hitting the exact spot every time. Just as I'd proclaimed it absolutely perfect, Rick arrived on Tsar.

"Nice one, Troy," he said approvingly. "You must have a real good teacher to have improved so much."

"Emma's a total star." Troy slid to the ground and patted Crystal. "And so is this pony. Between them they're making even a complete klutz like me look like something of a prince."

"Absolutely. Are you finished with the stage now? I need to put Tsar through the final routine."

"Sure," Troy said, and I added eagerly, "Please, can I watch?"

"Okay." Rick moved the black horse away to give instructions to a couple of crew members and I saw the other two who'd been working on the stage's top platform pack up their tools and leave.

Troy had already told me that at the climax of the battle in the last scene Rick would ride Tsar along the narrow platform that towered above the stage. Then he'd pluck the ceremonial Shushawny sabre from a flaming mountain peak and hold it aloft to signify victory. It sounded fairly simple but knowing Baz and his creative direction, I knew the whole thing would be spectacular. Rick entered from the left, cleaving his way through what would be battling warriors, then jumping Tsar through a huge hoop of fire to land at center stage, where the horse reared, silhouetted by the flames. They climbed up the long platform, which signified the Path

107

of Truth in the story, horse and rider going higher and higher till they reached the peak. This, like the hoop, would be burning fiercely, and the effect for the audience as their eyes were drawn to the black and silver horse at the flaming apex would be stunning. Even without flames, lights, or costume it was quite something to watch and I gasped several times as Tsar forged his way to the topmost platform. With a triumphant swoop Rick reached up and drew out a gleaming sabre and Tsar reared in a full pesade, his magnificent head level with the burning mountain peak in the background. Rick waved the sabre triumphantly at his prince.

"I'll be up on the fourth level doing my heroic act," Troy said. "Rick wants to get Tsar's performance right before we do it together – it's going to be great, isn't it?"

"Amazing," I said, and as Rick and the black horse descended, we applauded and cheered them.

"Thanks, but I don't think it was smooth enough," Rick said and called to the crew, "We go again, okay?"

"We'd better leave him to it." Troy started leading Crystal to the rear of the stage. "I wouldn't know how to teach a horse to do any of that. How does he get Tsar to rear for a start – it doesn't hurt the horse does it?"

"Not at all." I didn't like to say how easy it had been to train Rocco in the pesade and many other "airs above the ground" movements. "You can't get a horse to do anything he's not physically capable of.

Still holding Crystal's reins, Troy gave me a one-armed hug "I suppose you're right, but I can't believe the stuff you Pony Club kids are capable of. Whatever Baz asks for, you all just go ahead and do it!"

"Well it's the kind of thing we do all the time in mounted games. It was clever of Baz to recruit team members because we practice all the things he wants the tribes to do all the time. We neck-rein our ponies around poles, do barrel, rope, and pyramid racing, pick up flags, gallop, jump, and vault – even dress up in the Pony Club Games competitions."

"Dress up?" he looked disbelieving and I smiled sadly, thinking of Robert and I winning the bride and groom race only a few weeks before.

"Sure, though nothing as exotic as the Fantasy costumes."

"You're all going to look wonderful, even that long skinny boy who fell off this morning."

"Darren? Have you heard how he's doing?"

"He seems okay. Nothing broken, but Baz says he's limping and still moaning a lot. Between us I think he's hoping Darren will pull out of the play. Baz was on the point of getting rid of him when the accident happened."

"I'm not surprised; he's the worst Pony Club rider I've ever seen." I hesitated. "So they think it was definitely an accident this morning? When they stopped rehearsal and started checking the arena again we all thought it was another case of sabotage."

"No, Baz had to clear everyone out and check, but this time there was no foul play." Troy let Crystal stretch her neck and nibble the grass. "I hear there's been more trouble at your hotel, though."

I wasn't sure whether to talk about it. "When we got back someone else's room had been ransacked."

"So I heard. They're saying it was the kid who hurt his head, but Baz doesn't think so."

"Really?" I was quite startled. "Why?"

"Because there must be a connection to all the other booby traps and mishaps that have been going on. It started before the bunch of you came, so how could it be this kid making all the trouble?"

"That's true." I was enormously relieved Robert wasn't a suspect in Baz's eyes, but aware he was still guilty in the minds of all the Pony Club kids. "What does Baz think the motive is?"

"He – oh here he comes. Let's get practicing, quick."

I thought it was quite funny, the way Troy, like everyone else, seemed half scared of the bossy little director, but I obligingly started going through another of Troy's entrances. Baz, as it happened, wasn't aiming for us at all. We soon heard him at the front of the stage, talking Rick and Tsar through each step of the play's finale. I helped Troy practice a few more vaults, then had to leave for the field and the tribespeople rehearsal. Troy insisted on giving me a lift and I rode behind him again, but made him stop well before we got to the paddock so that Robert wouldn't see us together.

The rehearsal went well, the entrances and exits were going with precision and everyone seemed to be enjoying themselves. All except Robert, who still wore an expression of sullen gloom. I told myself I should try harder to get through to him, and wondered if the news that Baz believed someone else was responsible for all the trouble might do the trick. Once we'd finished for the day I rode Rocco across the field to the Zardonnes group and more or less hunted Robert down, cantering alongside Juniper and yelling until Rob reluctantly brought the gray to a halt.

"What do you want, Emma?" he turned his head and looked at me, his eyes cold and hard.

I quickly gabbled out what I'd heard, hoping desperately to see a gleam of *something* warm that horrible, frozen expression.

Instead he shrugged with complete disinterest and said, "Who cares what Baz thinks? Haven't you heard? Darren's parents are going to sue him for their son's injury and demand that the play be stopped. We'll all be sent home and as far as I'm concerned, it can't happen soon enough."

Chapter Twelve

There didn't seem to be anything to say to that, and I didn't move when Robert cantered swiftly away. It seemed I was wasting my time trying to get through to him so I just sat there until Rocco stamped a hoof and shook his head impatiently as he watched his friend leave the field.

"You don't understand why Juniper's gone without you," I said dully. "It's not your fault, Rocco. It's me Rob hates and there's nothing I can do about it."

My pony shook his head again, jerking the reins from my hands and then, taking me completely by surprise, took off across the field, causing me to bump myself on the back of the saddle and lose both stirrups. For a couple of seconds we tore across the grass, with me fumbling around like an idiot until I came to my senses and regained reins, irons, and control. Rocco responded at once, dropping obediently from flat out gallop in the sort of perfect downward transition you'd expect from a properly schooled pony.

"What the heck was that?" I asked him in disbelief. "There was no noise, nothing spooked you. Nothing ever does, so why did you run away with me like that?"

The black horse came to a precise halt and turned his head. Honestly, you have never seen a pony try so hard to talk as Rocco did at that moment. I stroked his neck gently wishing I could understand him. We'd covered quite a lot of ground, leaving the other kids far behind at the other end of the field. We were now near the gate that Robert had gone through.

"You want to follow Juniper?"

I know, I know, it seems pretty crazy to be sitting on my pony asking him questions, but Rocco so rarely misbehaves I felt I had to find out what he wanted.

Now, although I didn't give him the go-ahead, he walked eagerly to the gate and stood beside it, perfectly positioned for me to lean over and open it. I was still hesitant; if I rode through and we caught up with Robert what exactly was I supposed to say? Rocco pawed the ground again and even nudged the gate with his nose.

"Okay, okay, I'll worry about that if we find him."

I leaned over and clicked the gate open, holding the top bar as Rocco neatly stepped beyond it, turning immediately so I could swing the gate shut behind us. We were now on the outskirts of the park and beyond us was a high perimeter fence with a guard sitting beside another gate of the heavy metal, top-security kind. I said hello and asked if he'd seen anyone leave.

"A tall kid on a gray horse went through just now." He was obviously only interested in stopping anyone trying to get *in* to the park. "Are you leaving as well?"

Rocco quivered underneath me and I nodded. Once out in the open, Rocco waited till I gave him the aid for canter, then surged joyfully forward, his pounding hooves eating up the ground beneath us. Soon we'd left

Adventure World far behind, the terrain now rough countryside without any sign of fences or buildings. After days of short bursts of riding in the artificial surroundings of the Theme Park it was good to be cantering the long winding track. I had no idea where we were heading. I'd just decided to trust Rocco and let him follow his instinct.

The ground rose steeply and Rocco cantered easily uphill, ears pricked forward. We crested the hill and the ground leveled out, stretching before us in gently undulating curves. I saw too, why Rocco was looking so excited. A few minutes ahead of us a gray shape moved easily along the rough track and I knew my clever pony had found his friend, Juniper. Rocco, although back to his obedient self, was obviously dying to speed up. I gave him the signal and felt the surge of power as he lengthened into gallop. He flew across the coarse grass like a beautiful black bird and despite still having no idea what I was going to say when we reached Robert, I felt my heart lift with the excitement of the moment.

Ahead of us, Juniper turned his head and whinnied, the rushing wind carrying his call clearly through the air. Rocco kept galloping and Rob's head turned too, and I saw with relief that he slowed his pony, bringing him down to walk. Rocco and I were soon alongside them, where we slithered to a halt. Rocco stretched his neck and nuzzled Juniper gently, and for a moment their two heads rested together in greeting. I wish I could say that Robert and I followed suit by throwing ourselves into each other's arms but although we didn't do that, his dark eyes were full of concern rather than sullen contempt.

114

"What is it, Emma? Are you all right? Is someone ill?"

I realized it must have looked as though I was on some kind of emergency mission and I gulped nervously, still unable to come up with anything to say.

"Emma!" He leaned forward and his face was the face I'd known all along, kind and loving and handsome. "What's wrong?"

I'm usually pretty even-tempered but the last few days of pent-up emotion had become too much and suddenly I was sobbing.

His eyes widened in surprise and he said awkwardly, "Don't cry, Em. You never cry."

"Well I am now!" It was true, the tears were absolutely pouring down my face and he brushed them gently away.

"Come and sit down over here." He slid off Juniper's back and held my reins while I scrambled clumsily to the ground.

I'd had no idea I was going to cry, but now that I'd started I just couldn't stop. I bawled like a little kid, sobbing incoherently about the jealousy I felt about Rob's feelings for Trudy, the distress of hearing the accusations against him, and the fear that all he felt for me was hatred. Robert was really sweet, sitting as close as he could while holding the horses' reins hooked through one arm and hugging me tight with the other. Eventually my sobs became occasional hiccups, and he tilted my chin so I'd look up into his face.

"Are you really crying because you think I hate you?"

I nodded. "I – just wanted you to talk to me."

"And you came galloping out here just to get me to do that?"

I decided not to mention it had actually been Rocco's idea to follow him. I figured Robert would like it a lot more if he thought it came from me alone. There wasn't much chance of my horse snitching on me, so I nodded.

"Oh Emma!" he hugged me again. "I thought you didn't give a darn about me since Troy Mitchell hit the scene."

"He's not on *my* scene, I keep telling you that." I wiped my eyes with a very soggy tissue.

"But I saw the way he looked at you, and after everything Trudy said –"

"Trudy!" I interrupted furiously. "Can't you see *she's* the one who's responsible for breaking us up?

"Why would she do that?" Rob looked genuinely puzzled and I sighed.

"I'll spell it out for you, okay? She likes you for herself, it was obvious from that very first night."

He was silent for a moment. "But she told me it was *you* who liked Troy. And when you started going off with him all the time I thought it must be true. I was so jealous, Emma."

Knowing what a horrible experience it was to feel like that, my voice softened. "I *told* you I was helping him with his riding. You should have believed me, Rob."

"I tried." He hung his head. "But every time I saw you together I thought Trudy must be right. She's known plenty of people like you who ditched their old friends when someone better came along."

"Trudy might act that way but you should know I don't. Did she tell you your dad didn't really want you around as well?"

"I was upset that first night because he didn't come to

117

see me like he promised," Robert said slowly. "The next day he explained that he'd been bogged down with work, but Trudy said when her dad left he used to make the same kind of excuses. Now she figures he only takes her out when he wants to upset her mother."

"Well if that's true it's no wonder she's such a destructive witch." I looked into his eyes. "But can't you see what she said just isn't true of your own dad? He genuinely wanted you here so he could spend time with you, but you won't let him in. And now there's all this suspicion about you stealing and you won't even talk to him about it. All you want to do is run."

"There didn't seem any point in either talking or staying." He'd dropped his eyes and was staring moodily at the ground. "I thought everyone had decided I was no good, and if you and Dad had given up on me there was no reason to stay."

"How many times do I have to tell you I would never give up on you? And neither would your dad."

He raised his head, his expression so hopeful and vulnerable I wanted to kiss him.

"Honest? And you don't want Troy for your boyfriend?"

"Honest." I did kiss him then, but only softly on the cheek and his face brightened so much I added, "I thought I already *had* a boyfriend, Robert."

"You do, Emma, I promise you do."

This time our lips actually met and it would have been a wonderful moment if Rocco hadn't decided to wander off, his reins wrenching Robert's arm so that he slid flat on his back along the grass. Still, as romantic beginnings go, it was pretty encouraging and I felt a million times happier as I got up to disentangle Robert from my pony's reins. We rode back toward Adventure World, keeping the pace slow to cool the horses, and it was wonderful to be together and in tune with each other once again. As soon as we'd settled Rocco and Juniper for the night we went over to Space World to wait for Alan. The tightened security measures meant we weren't allowed in, but as soon as Robert saw his dad's car he ran over to greet him. Alan's face was more drawn and worried than ever, but I saw an immediate glimmer of joy when his son started talking. I thought they should have some time alone, but they both insisted I join them for an evening meal in a restaurant in town. They certainly had a lot to talk about and I was pleased to know Alan's belief in his son's integrity was completely unshaken.

"I told Baz there was no way you'd be stealing. He didn't take much convincing really, and said he'd already figured there must be a connection to all the other stuff going on. I'm afraid most of the other kids have decided you're the thief but that's based on circumstantial evidence."

"They don't know Rob the way we do," I agreed and Robert squeezed my hand under the table and smiled at me in that lovely new/old way of his. "What we should do," I went on, "is find out who really did steal the money from the hotel."

"I'm hoping Baz and his team will discover who's behind the trouble" Alan said. "Once the saboteur's been exposed, I'm sure he'll turn out to be the thief as well. Baz is refusing to abandon rehearsals, by the way, despite the threat from Darren's parents to sue him."

"As long as you two know I'm innocent, that's good

enough," Robert said quietly. "And Baz, I suppose. I've been so depressed I haven't given him or his play my best shot, but if it's going ahead and he's okay with my staying, I'll try to do a lot better."

"That's a brave decision to make," Alan told him. "You're probably in for a hard time from the other kids."

"Mostly only Trudy and her friends," Robert said. "I think Fox and the others are holding off till there's real proof."

"If Fox truly thought you'd swiped his cash he'd have decked you by now," I said candidly. "He's not very big but he's fiery."

They both laughed and I thought how good it was for all three of us to be together like this. The nice, relaxed feeling lasted all the way back to Adventure World and our hotel. Alan came in with us to make sure there there would be no trouble. I also braced myself for any unpleasantness we might encounter. As always, it seemed, we were greeted by a hubbub of speculation and unrest. It was nothing to do with Robert, though. Late that afternoon the saboteur had struck again, and this time he'd caused a problem that even Baz was going to find impossible to overcome.

Rick, the number one stunt man and the wonderful, peerless Tsar, had both been injured. They were all right and would live to perform another day, but their appearance in the Fantasy play was definitely ruled out. The buzz of excited, outraged conversation in the big games room had only one theme. Had the saboteur really won, and was the troubled Fantasy Play finally going to be cancelled?

Chapter Thirteen

It was Fox, with his insider knowledge gained from the stunt riders, who told us all about it.

"Rick went back to the arena on his own to rehearse some more. There was a security guard up there, but Rick sent him off to get a prop he needed and started practicing the part he does on the high platform. He and Tsar did it twice with no problem, then the guard came back with the hoop Rick wanted and they fiddled around with it on the bottom level of the stage."

"I've seen this part," I said. "But Rick usually has crew members to help him."

"I guess there weren't any around," Fox said. "Anyway, after a while he was satisfied with that and he said he'd go through the whole ride just once more. Tsar jumped through the hoop okay and started climbing the platform. Before he reached the top he stumbled really badly and threw Rick over his head. Luckily he didn't fly over the platform railing – they say if he'd landed on one of the lower levels he'd have broken his back. As it is he's got a badly sprained ankle and a broken wrist."

"How awful!" I was shocked. "And what about Tsar? Poor Rick will be more concerned about his horse being hurt."

"Luckily Tsar didn't panic and they were able to lead him down from the platform so it could have been a lot worse. He's completely lame but the vet says it's not too serious and he'll be sound after a few weeks' box rest."

"How did it happen?" Alan wanted to know. "Did someone sneak up there and throw oil around again?"

"No, but while Rick and the guard were busy at the front of the stage somebody climbed up the rigging at the rear and pushed a piece of metal through the back of the high platform. It blended in so Rick and his horse wouldn't have known it was there until Tsar hit his leg against it and stumbled."

"Whoever did that should be shot!" Robert said furiously. "It could have killed them both!"

Fox turned a wary eye on him. "Trudy was saying you were missing after rehearsal. I hope you've got an alibi because she wants to blame you for everything that happens now I think."

"Stupid cow!" Now it was my turn to be angry. "Robert was with me, nowhere near the arena, and I'll be glad to tell her so."

"Look, Fox," Robert faced him directly. "I know it looks bad for me the way Stuart's money disappeared, but I swear I didn't have anything to do with that or the other stuff that was stolen. And as for setting up traps to injure anybody – you've got to believe me. I just couldn't do a thing like that."

"Alice said that too. Although you've been a miserable creep since you've been here, I've never thought of you as a crook," Fox said bluntly. "Though I think you should do something about proving it."

"We intend to," I said quickly. "But if Rick's fall means the play's being cancelled, we don't have much time."

"I think we should start by talking to Baz," Robert said. "I want to thank him for believing my dad when he said I wasn't guilty and tell him there might still be a way we can save his play."

"That would be great." Despite all the traumas, I still meant it. "But what do you mean?"

"Dad, could you take us over to Baz's hotel please?" Rob looked very purposeful and Alan and I found ourselves trotting to keep up with him as we went back to the car.

The other hotel was a ten-minute drive away, and as soon as we set off I repeated my question.

"How are you planning to stop the play from being cancelled, Robert?"

"Well ..." He looked out at the darkening mass of Horror Wood. "It could only be with triple security so there's absolutely no possibility of any more 'accidents'."

"I'm sure Baz would go along with that," Alan said. "But what are you saying? Who would take Rick's part? Another stunt man?"

"That wouldn't work – the rider who travels the platform to free the Sushawny sabre has got to be on a black and silver horse. It's in the story and they've spent a fortune portraying it around the roller coaster."

"That's right," I agreed. "The computer-generated horse that rears above the ride and flails his silver hooves

123

is jet black with silver flashes. "That's why only Tsar – "
I stopped abruptly and Robert squeezed my hand.

"Only Tsar – or Rocco," he said quietly and there was
a terrible grinding noise as Alan crunched the car's gears
in alarm.

"You don't mean you're going to suggest Emma does
it? She's told me all about that finale and even without a
maniac tripping the horse, it's a dangerous piece of riding."

"Emma and Rocco could do it," Rob said with complete confidence. "They can do absolutely anything together."

I was getting over the shock and thinking it through.
"We could jump through the hoop onto the stage, that's
easy, and I'm pretty sure Rocco will be fine when it's on
fire – "

There was another crunching noise and Alan said
faintly, "The thing's on *fire*?"

"Yes." In my mind I was riding the route I'd seen
Rick and Tsar complete. "Climbing the roller coaster
platform won't be a problem even though we've never
gone that high before. Like you say, Rocco's so brave
he'll do it."

"Your horse isn't the only one who's brave." Alan
brought the car to a stop and turned to look at me. "Are
you sure you want to do this, Emma?"

I was absolutely sure and couldn't wait to put the idea
to Baz. We found him in a big, cluttered room that was
crammed with technical equipment.

"Come in." He sounded worn out and listless, all his
bounce and energy gone.

Robert plunged right in, explaining how despite appearances, he was innocent of the hotel thefts, and thanking Baz for thinking so.

"It's your father you should thank," Baz replied wearily. "I knew any kid whose dad feels the way yours does about you must be all right. The stealing from the hotel was just one more thing to force me to cancel, and the real culprit either tried to make it look like you were guilty or it was just a coincidence – you were in the wrong place at the wrong time."

"Thanks for seeing it like that." Robert hesitated. "And – um – sorry I haven't given my best. I was a bit messed up but I'll be going all-out from now on."

"Good of you, Robert, but I think you're a bit late with that. I've battled this madman, whoever he is, every step of the way. This time I think he's won. Rick and Tsar aren't the big name stars, but their last scene is the one the whole Fantasy is based around. That image of the black and silver horse rearing against a background of flames is the symbol of the story. Jim and the other guys volunteered to do the finale but they just don't have the look, and it's only a few days to opening night – far too late to find another black horse."

"You don't have to." My voice sounded a bit squeaky even to me. "Rocco's black and he's got the same kind of presence as Tsar and he's only a bit smaller."

Baz's jaw dropped and he stared at me. "Who the heck's – you mean *your* horse?"

"Yes," I said, more firmly this time. "I've seen the finale routine and we can do it."

"We? You mean *you'd* ride him?" The little director was now perched on the very edge of his chair.

"Of course I would." I didn't actually say, "Just let

125

anyone else try," but he got the message. "You won't even have to alter the costume. Rick's broader than I, but not much taller."

"But – but – " he was practically falling on the floor. "It's complicated, dangerous and – "

"Rocco and I can do it," I repeated and turned to Robert and Alan. "Can't we?"

They both nodded vigorously and Baz gripped the edge of his desk, staring at us.

"Just try us out in the morning," I said while he was still speechless. "If you don't like us you can go ahead and cancel."

"But Baz, all security will have to be tripled so there's no chance of a repeat of today's trouble." Alan was still worrying and the director nodded.

I got up quickly. "See you tomorrow, Baz. What time would you like?"

"Six a.m." He was still absolutely stunned. "Please."

"Okay." Robert opened the door for me and we walked back across the hotel lobby.

"That was – " He began, but his words were lost. From behind us someone gave a great shout and I suddenly felt myself being picked up and twirled around. It could only be Troy, and as I turned to face him I just hoped Alan had the sense to get a good grip on Robert and either stop him from walking out or slugging the actor.

"Emma!" Troy's handsome face was very close to mine. "I was just coming over to find you so we could say goodbye. Have you heard the news about Rick?"

"That's why we're here." Robert stepped firmly between us, his dark head towering above our own. "So there's no need for any goodbyes."

126

"Oh?" Troy backed off immediately, looking a bit scared.

"I'm going to try riding the finale," I explained rapidly. "Hopefully, Baz won't have to cancel."

"Well I'm all for that but Emma, darling, it's too dangerous– "

"Emma darling will be fine." Robert's arm was now protectively around me, and poor Troy blinked in bewilderment.

"Come and watch me in the morning." I smiled at him as Rob started marching toward the front door.

"Wow!" Alan said as he unlocked the car. "It's just as well Troy's fan club didn't see that! You practically wiped the floor with the poor guy, Robert!"

"He shouldn't be so free with his cuddles and his darlings then," Rob growled and I punched his arm quite hard.

"Hey, don't you start going all moody again."

His dark eyes softened as soon as he looked at me. "I'm not mad at you, Em, I just think Troy Mitchell needs to be straightened out about a few things, that's all."

I just couldn't be mad at him, so I snuggled in close on the car seat and thought how none of the other girls would believe it felt so much better being hugged by Robert than the glamorous Troy Mitchell. Troy was a lovely guy though, and when Rocco and I turned up at the arena the next morning, his was the first face I saw.

"Emma!" He still looked worried as he came to stand beside us. "I've told Baz I think he's crazy to put you through this. One of the stunt guys should ride Rocco."

"No way." I was feeling nervous and sounded snappier than I meant. "Rocco wouldn't do it for anyone else, so it's me or no one."

Robert, watching from the side, started moving toward us and Troy quickly backed away. I walked to the center, and I calmed myself down by doing some basic dressage with Rocco until Baz called me over to give his last-minute instructions. To be honest, I hardly heard. My mind was now completely focused on the task ahead and soon I was cantering away to begin my entrance for the finale.

We rode into the arena from the left, remembering to curve a line through the "battlefield," and then cantered a perfect straight line toward the stage. The hoop was in place, unlit, since this was my first run-through. It still needed a precise approach in order to leap through it successfully. Rocco, of course, thought it very exciting and popped over like an old hand, to pivot and bend his haunches in the classic pesade – rearing on his hind legs in exactly the right spot to be silhouetted within the circular frame of the hoop. Nothing to worry about there. Now came the ascent onto the high platform. Rocco traversed the second and third levels in great style and hesitated only for a moment when his hooves clattered onto the steeply ascending platform. I remembered once riding him across a slender wooden bridge that many of the other ponies had refused, and I encouraged him forward, trying to instill in him the confidence he needed. He responded at once and we climbed higher and higher, moving effortlessly along the narrow, difficult roller coaster as if it were the most normal thing in the world. As we reached the apex I stood in my stirrups and reached for the sabre, plucking it out of the mountain of flames in the dramatic way I'd seen Rick do it. As I held it triumphantly aloft, Rocco reared again, holding the stance and thrashing his forelegs, and I heard a spontaneous cheer break out from the people watching far below us. All that was left was the descent, an easier route without the theatrical twists and turns we'd had to maneuver on the way up. Then I was handing the sabre to Baz.

"It's heavier than I thought," I said. "Made my arm ache a bit."

He burst out laughing and carried on till I thought he'd choke, so I climbed out of my saddle and waited for him to stop.

"Emma, you were – you were absolutely wonderful," he spluttered at last.

"Thank you, but I'd like to try it with the battle going on below us please, just so Rocco knows what to expect."

The little man, all his enthusiasm restored, bounced immediately away and soon everyone was rushing around getting a full rehearsal organized. I saw Robert go tearing down the hill to get Juniper ready and as soon as he was gone, Troy emerged from the Wardrobe trailer and ran to me.

"You were sensational." He put his arms out but I was too quick and managed to duck out of the way.

"Thanks Troy, but you'd better ease up on the hugging. I don't want my boyfriend ruining everything after all this by giving you a black eye."

"Ah." He was silent for a moment. "Your boyfriend. I didn't realize you had one, Emma."

"Well we've had a bit of a rough time lately, but we're

fine now. I'm really sorry, Troy, but Robert thinks you like me and he's a bit jealous. Silly I know, but – "

"It's not silly." To my amazement his usually smiling face was very sad. "I *do* like you – a lot – but I won't mess up your life if it's Robert you want to be with."

He turned away and I watched him walk slowly back to the trailer, leaving me alone and frankly, gobsmacked!

Chapter Fourteen

By the time Baz hurtled back I'd just about recovered from the shock. The next couple of hours were so intense I didn't get time to think about anything except the play. While everyone was getting ready, Rocco and I practiced our hoop-jumping-platform-climbing scene, perfecting the pace and the timing till it was flawless. The director needed to make sure my pony would be all right with the fire on stage so he arranged a trial run with the special effects crew who got it all going under strictly enforced safety regulations. As I'd thought, Rocco was completely unfazed by the flames and did the whole routine like a pro.

"Amazing," Jim kept saying "Absolutely amazing!"

"Not really," I told him, a bit out of breath from all my sabre waving. "Rocco's always come along when we have a bonfire at home and he hates to miss a party. He joins me at barbecues and firework displays too."

That made Baz start laughing again and, while I was glad to cheer him up, I couldn't really see why he found the things my horse and I did together so funny. Once the actors arrived and took their places there was a great

buzz of anticipation and when the tribespeople came cantering up the hill to join us I could almost feel the excitement that filled the air. This was our first complete run-through and although Baz, bouncing up and down on his rostrum, called out directions and let out the occasional howl when something went wrong, he allowed us to complete the whole of the first act without stopping. He'd told me this was to rekindle all the confidence and enthusiasm that had been sucked out of everyone by the problems. Now, once Troy had made his dramatic speech and the Sushawny tribe performed their warrior-like display for their elders, it was intermission time and actors and tribespeople milled around behind the stage, sounding very pleased and animated. It was just the reaction Baz had been hoping for, and before he sent us off for a break he told everyone we were doing great and he was proud to be involved with us.

"Hah!" I laughed to Alice and Fox. "Wait till later and he starts nit-picking again."

"D'you think he will?" Alice was lying flat out on the grass while Paint grazed placidly beside her. "I was hoping he hadn't noticed the way I crashed into one of those mystic trees we have to bend round."

"He noticed," I said with conviction. "He's just being gentle with us this morning, me especially. Did you see the mess I made of my sabre twirl? "

"You're doing great." Fox looked hot and sweaty. "Apart from the couple of stunts Jim took over, you're doing all the stuff Rick and Tsar were performing."

"Emma's a star, didn't you know?" Alice waved a lazy hand at him. "Would you get the star and me an ice cream to cool us down, Foxy?"

"Sure." He went off immediately and I raised my eyebrows.

"Foxy? I'm surprised he lets you call him that."

"I can do what I like, he's crazy about me," Alice said complacently. "Speaking of which, what exactly did you do to turn Robert back into a devoted admirer and genuine nice guy? I've never seen such a change; you must have said something amazing!"

"I got him to tell me what that cat Trudy had been saying to him. He'd been feeling pretty insecure and she worked on that, telling him lies about his dad and Troy and me. Once he knew the truth he realized who his real friends are."

She noticed the pause and pounced immediately. "Friend? You mean girlfriend don't you? Has he asked you to go out with him at last?"

"Don't be nosey." I looked away and spotted someone in the crowd. "Hey, isn't that Darren over there? I thought his parents would have taken him away by now."

"They're on vacation – they did some threatening by phone but can't collect him yet, so he's just going to watch," Alice said rapidly. "Don't change the subject. So you and Robert are officially a couple, are you? What does he say about hunky Troy and his kisses and cuddles?"

I really, really didn't want to talk about that and was extremely glad that Fox had come back with the ice cream.

"I've been thinking." He handed them over. "Now that we're staying, we really ought to figure out who else could have stolen Stuart's money. The other thefts could have been anyone, but I think Robert's still having a bad time with Trudy and her pals because they think he's the only one who could be guilty."

"Alan says Baz won't rest till he finds out who injured Rick and did all the other stuff." I slurped the ice cream gratefully. "Maybe then we'll have the thief as well."

"Don't see how." Fox frowned. "No one else went into the hotel and every single kid except Robert was at rehearsal."

"So the guards say." Alice, I was glad to see, was firmly back on Robert's side. "But maybe they're the ones who are lying. The trouble started before we got here, Troy told Emma."

"It's very complicated." I gave the last bit of ice cream to Rocco. "First to go wrong were things like mistakes in the equipment ordered, and while that was being sorted out, the stage was vandalized. Then we arrived and the thefts at the hotel began."

"It's as though there's a whole gang of people trying to stop the play," Alice agreed. "Oh look, here comes lover boy!"

For an embarrassing moment I thought she'd guessed about Troy, but thank goodness it was Robert who was approaching.

"Hi." I jumped up to greet him. "Baz told us to stay in our tribes till the break's over, so I didn't think you'd come over."

"I just wanted to see a friendly face, especially yours." Rob tipped my chin up and smiled into my eyes. "I'm not exactly flavor of the month with the Zardonnes."

"I bet that's Trudy and her big mouth," I said angrily. "Ignore her, Robert."

"I'll try, though actually it's Stuart who's doing most

135

of the bad-mouthing." Rob patted Rocco affectionately, trying to be cheerful. "You're doing great, young man. Just make sure you look after Emma for me."

"I should be all right." I pointed at the people around us. "The security staff are practically outnumbering the rest of us, so I don't think anyone will dare try producing another 'accident'."

He put his arm around me and we went for a little walk, eventually crossing the arena together until we reached the far side where the Zardonne tribe was resting. Robert gave me a brief hug as he left me to join them, and I watched anxiously as he went over to get Juniper. I saw Stuart and Trudy turn their backs, but Ginny smiled at him and Jake handed over his pony's reins in friendly fashion. I was glad not everyone was against him. Once the intermission break was over we carried on with our run-through. The second act went pretty well too, though there were a few mistakes that would have to be rectified and I knew Baz would get us all working hard to get the whole play running perfectly by opening night.

The last finale was already a brilliant success. Troy was a wonderful prince as he battled with the Zardonne leader in an amazing display of swordsmanship and heroics. A few of the girls forgot to be warriors for a minute or two, being so distracted by watching Troy up there on the stage. I was slightly nervous about my own entrance on the battlefield but Rocco, as always, was superb, forging his way through the fighting to make his fantastic ascent of the burning platform. Baz was kind, telling everyone how proud he was and instructing us to take a good, long break before he started what he always called "honing" individual performances.

"My performance doesn't need so much honing as throwing away completely," Alice moaned as we rode back to the paddock. "I was awful and it's all your fault, Emma."

"Me!" I said, "What did I do?"

"Nothing much, just leapt through fire and climbed up a burning mountain." She glared at me. "I nearly fell off in the finale I was so scared for you."

"Don't be," I said lightly. "It's fun."

She rolled her eyes and pretended to faint and Robert, who'd joined us, laughed in sympathy and said, "I felt the same, Alice, in fact much worse, probably."

"Ah well, that's love for you," she said wickedly, but instead of denying it like he used to, Rob just winked.

There was no need for them to worry about any sabotage though, because it was obvious over the next day or so that security levels were at an all-time high. There were guards everywhere, at the hotel, the paddocks and particularly the arena. All our rehearsals were now being held there. Although every aspect was again subjected to Baz's eagle eye and there was far more stopping and starting, they were still enjoyable. Opening night was now only a day away, nothing had gone wrong and we were all really excited at the prospect of the full dress rehearsal. It was almost magical seeing the transformation. While the actors got into costume and had their make-up done, all us Pony Club kids got our horses ready, with the help of the design crew and wardrobe staff. The Sushawny ponies looked fabulous with beaded headdresses and sparkling colored ribbons plaited into their manes and tails. The Zardonne horses weren't all bejeweled and glamorous but they looked incredibly menacing draped in flowing panels of somber-colored mesh.

"Look at Juniper!" Alice wound the band fixing the last streamer in Paint's mane. "He looks like a dangerous jousting horse about to go into combat."

"Robert said when he put the coat on Juniper the first time he loved it. Thought he had a fancy new anti-sweat rug and wanted to roll in it!" I laughed, watching the skilled way Rocco's silver flashes were being applied. "In fact all the horses seem excited today – I think they like dressing up as much as we do."

When we all assembled in the arena I couldn't hear myself think above the incredible racket of talking and laughing and general excitement. I sat on Rocco and watched the other kids getting off their ponies and running around taking photos of each other and the actors and generally creating absolute mayhem. Most of them wanted pictures taken with Troy who looked magnificent in his white and gold prince's panoply. Crystal, her long white mane and tail shot through with gold, was also a stunning sight and the pair of them glittered from the tip of Crystal's hooves to the jewels in Troy's royal crown. The TV star was, as ever, very good-natured about having countless pictures taken and chatted away to his fans for what seemed an eternity. I wondered why Baz wasn't calling for the pandemonium to end and the dress rehearsal to begin. Then I noticed a lot of activity going on amongst the security guards. The news soon spread that there had been another sabotage attempt and my heart sank at the thought that the play might, after all this, be cancelled and our hard work wasted.

"It's all right!" Fox had the latest update. "They

caught someone trying to tamper with the flame burning equipment and they got him before he could do any damage."

"He could have hurt Emma!" Alice went quite pale, and I must admit I felt suddenly sick myself. "Who is it Fox, do we know him?"

"They're putting him in that car over there, look!" He pointed and we craned our necks to see.

"It's one of the crew," I said, still feeling shaky. "The tall, skinny one."

"I can't see over the crowd," Alice complained and I peered again.

"He usually wears a blue cap – you know the guy we saw in town – the one you said reminded you of some-one."

"Oh yeah." She was still trying to catch a glimpse of the man surrounded by security guards. "I'm really glad they got him, though I don't see how *he* could have done the thefts at the hotel."

The car was leaving, pulling out slowly with the sabo-teur pinned safely between two guards. As he turned his head to look at the arena I suddenly did a classic double take.

"I've got it! That crewman didn't do the stealing – he got someone else to do it and I know who! Quick. I've got to tell Security!"

Alice and Fox helped me push my way through the crowd and find a guard. He listened attentively and said I should follow him to one of the trailers, so I jumped off Rocco and handed his reins to Alice. Inside the trailer Baz was on the phone, surrounded by his assistants who were all looking shocked but relieved.

"Emma!" the director came toward me. "You've heard what's happened? Don't worry, you aren't in any danger – the maniac didn't do any damage, I promise."

"I know, I'm fine with that. It's not why I'm here. Baz, that crewman you've just arrested – he's got an accomplice."

"What?" he stopped dead. "How do you – who the heck is it?"

"I think it's his son. Alice spotted the resemblance first, but the rest of us couldn't see it. The crewman always wore a baseball cap but I've just seen him without it and there's no doubt who he looks like – it's Darren!"

"You mean the skinny kid who hurt his leg? But he was recruited like the rest of you; he's a bona fide Pony Club member. It can't be him, Emma. His parents phoned me and threatened to sue and – " he stopped abruptly, his brain working overtime. "You know, I thought it was strange they were that angry and yet didn't break their vacation to come and pick him up." He turned to his staff. "Send someone out to find the kid Darren – NOW!"

As usual when Baz yelled there was an instant response and the security guard and two assistants rushed off immediately.

"While they're doing that," I ventured, "maybe you should come out and get everyone else calmed down. It's bedlam out there."

"And you want to get started, right?" Baz gave his great roar of laughter and patted me on the back. "You're a real professional, you know that?"

We walked out to the arena together and Baz started organizing everyone, lining the Sushawny to the left, the

140

Zardonnes to the right and the actors on stage in the middle. I felt a bit foolish having to plod across the center to reclaim Rocco, especially when halfway across, my silver boots, which were gradually slipping with every step, slithered right down and tangled around my feet. Troy, who was just about to ride to join his tribe for their entrance, spotted my problem, dismounted, and came back to help me. We re-fixed one of the boots and I was half in of the other when there was a sudden roar behind me and a wild figure burst out of the right-hand crowd and came sprinting toward us.

"It's your fault Emma, you witch!" Darren, his face contorted with fury, was barely recognizable. "They were going to cancel till you took over and we'd have done it! It was you who stopped us from getting our revenge!"

Struggling with the boot, I had no chance of running, and when Troy gave a sort of strangulated squeak and took off, leaving me alone, I felt very, very scared. There were guards chasing Darren but he had a good start and I could see they wouldn't reach him before he got to me. I wished I was holding the sabre of the Sushawny so I'd have a chance of defending myself but then, to my joy I saw the warrior horse with his brown-robed rider streaking like a tawny arrow toward Darren. He was so close I could see the madness gleam in his eyes, but as he flung out his arm to get me, Juniper caught up with him, and Robert, bending low in the saddle, swooped the running figure up. He cantered away to dump him unceremoniously on the ground at a safe distance from where I stood. The guards kept going, racing past me to pounce on Darren, as he lay huddled, but still ranting on the

grass. Robert turned Juniper and cantered back to me, instantly sliding from his horse to hold me protectively in his arms. Honestly, even after all the amazing scenes we'd rehearsed, it was just the most heroic, romantic thing I'd ever witnessed and I hugged him as tightly as our costumes would allow.

We did eventually get started on the dress rehearsal and as I took my place behind the prince of the Sushawny for our first entrance Troy leaned over and whispered shame-facedly, "Sorry I bolted and left you. Seems you made the right choice after all."

I had never doubted it for a minute, but there was no point in being hard on the lovely, cowardly, Troy.

"It's all right," I said lightly "You make a great stage hero."

He smiled ruefully and put Crystal into canter to lead his adoring tribe into the arena.

* * *

The next day, of course, was opening night, with all the excitement of our very first audience. My parents had come all the way to see me, and although I suffered horribly from stage fright at first, once we got going it was the best night of my life. The whole week was brilliant, spending all day with Robert and having a great time in the now fully-open Adventure World, and performing with my beautiful Rocco in the highly acclaimed Fantasy play every night.

It took a day or two for the full story of the attempted sabotage to come out. When it did, it left one vital point unanswered. It had been a well-planned and complex

143

plot, starting with the appointment of one Sally Benjamin at the agency that had booked Baz to direct Adventure World's opening. It was Sally who'd altered equipment orders, had the wrong things sent to the wrong places, and created mischief from the very start. She'd been very clever at covering her tracks and no one suspected that she'd also diverted a job offer away from a genuine crewman, getting her husband to take his place and join the crew where he could start his campaign of destruction and vandalism. In the same way, Sally also replaced one of the Pony Club kids with her son, getting him to play the part of Darren. He was the one who'd created further mayhem with the thefts at the hotel and the attempted arson in the wardrobe trailer.

"I should have known he wasn't the real Pony Club kid," Fox said. "There was just no way he was good enough to be a club team member."

"I always thought Trudy was a fake, personally," Alice commented. "She's terrible as well."

"Not really," Robert said thoughtfully. "Trudy's a drag and she's slow at learning new stuff but she *can* actually ride a horse. Don't you think that what this Sally Benjamin and her family did was diabolical, though? Has anyone come up with a reason why they wanted revenge on Baz so badly?"

"I have," I said slowly. "It was because they hate Baz and wanted him disgraced publicly and professionally. Over the top, I know, but I think the whole clan are completely off their rockers."

"What did he ever do to them?" Alice wanted to know. "It can't be just a personality thing, surely."

"The oldest son wanted to be an actor, but not only

was he awful, he was lazy and arrogant as well, and Baz told him so and fired him from something last year. Since then he's become a dropout and drifted into drugs and crime and his whole family, especially Sally, blames Baz. It was her plan to get back at him this way and she made sure her husband and son created hell for him."

"It must have been her on the phone when I heard 'Darren' getting nagged," Fox remembered. "She must be totally nuts to blame her son's failure on Baz. I know he can seem kind of terrifying but he's completely fair and honest. Well, nice though it is to have questions answered and loose ends tied up, there's one major piece left completely *untied*."

"I know what you mean," Robert said unhappily. "Even though we know this family did virtually all the troublemaking there's one crime they couldn't be responsible for, and that's the theft of Stuart's money. The fake Darren was being injured at rehearsal when the money was taken, and his father didn't go near the hotel at all. I guess it still looks as though there's only one person who could have done it, and that's me."

"Not exactly." I'd been thinking about this A LOT. "I want to try something – will you all back me up?"

"Sure," they agreed at once and we walked once more into the games room of the hotel.

There weren't too many kids around, but Ginny and her girlfriends were playing pool while Trudy showed off some new clothes to the ever-faithful Stuart. She saw us approaching and wrinkled her pretty nose.

"Ooh, nasty smell coming," she said cattily. "Stolen any more cash lately, Robert?"

He opened his mouth to reply and I said quickly, "I

145

thought you'd have heard from Security. They know Robert isn't guilty."

"Don't be stupid." Trudy stamped her foot. "I realize Darren stole the first time, but he couldn't have taken Stuart's money."

"That's true," I agreed. "But then, nobody could. Isn't that right, Stuart?"

"I don't know what you mean." He moved uneasily on the sofa.

"Well, they've checked, you see, and the money you said was in your room just couldn't have been there."

"Huh?" Trudy's blue eyes were puzzled.

"Stuart said he'd gotten some cash from his aunt, cash she sent by *mail*. But they've checked and he didn't get any mail that day – *none at all!*"

There was a moment's stunned silence, then Robert said slowly, "So he just made it *look* as though he'd been robbed, by emptying out drawers and throwing stuff around the room."

"That's right," I said. "Stuart did all that before he left in the morning, then he made sure his roommate went straight back to their room at lunchtime so he'd have a witness that it had been trashed."

"But – but – why?" Trudy turned to stare at him.

For a while Stuart tried to deny everything, blustering that we were making it all up. I stuck to my story determinedly, backed up strongly by Robert and the other two, and eventually, believing we were about to call Security, he broke down.

"I knew Robert was going to be alone in the hotel and I wanted him to get the blame," he admitted drearily. "You were getting too fond of him, Trudy, and I had to throw you off. If I made it look like he was the thief you'd think he took your necklace and I knew you'd never forgive him for that."

"Oh, *Stuart*!" Ginny and her gang had heard everything and I knew it wouldn't be long before all the other kids were told how Robert had been set up.

I hoped at the very least Stuart would apologize, but looking at his sulky expression I decided not to hold my breath. Trudy, of course, tried being sweet and flirtatious to Robert and I was really, *really* glad when he told her to get lost. My friends were very impressed at the way I'd trapped Stuart into a confession, especially when I admitted I hadn't known for sure if he'd received any mail that day – it was just a piece of inspired guesswork!

Clearing up that part of the mystery made the week absolutely perfect, now everyone knew for certain that Rob was no thief. The fact his dad had never doubted him had altered Rob's attitude completely, and he was once more the gorgeous, kind, laid-back guy he used to be – and best of all he was *my* boyfriend!

The last night of the Fantasy play arrived far too quickly but it ended on a high note with the audience literally going wild as they clapped, cheered, whistled, and stamped their feet in appreciation. The entire cast called Rocco and me forward to take a solo curtain call, and my wonderful black horse did his full thank-you routine, ending in the deepest of bows that brought everyone to their feet in a standing ovation. The after-show party was a riot with half the girls in floods of tears because the play was over and the other half dying to get home and show everyone their photos of Troy Mitchell. Troy himself had been a bit quiet, still embarrassed about the way

he'd run away from Darren, but as the party drew to a close, he took me to one side and handed me a little box.

"It's a thank-you present for all the help you gave me." His teeth gleamed in that fabulous grin. "I won't kiss you in case your boyfriend's looking, but I'll never forget you, Emma, and I hope we meet again one day. The little gift is something to remind you of the play. I hope you like it."

Very touched, I took out a fine gold chain threaded through the delicate figure of a rearing ebony horse whose perfect little hooves flashed pure silver. I knew I would keep it forever; a lasting memento of the time Rocco had been the most amazing Fantasy Horse.